The Miracle Tree

Demystifying the Qabalah

By
R. J. Stewart

New Page Books
A division of The Career Press, Inc.
Franklin Lakes, NJ

THE MIRACLE TREE
EDITED AND TYPESET BY NICOLE DEFELICE
COVER DESIGN BY THE VISUAL GROUP
Printed in the U.S.A. by Book-mart Press

To order this title, please call toll-free 1-800-CAREER-1 (NJ and Canada: 201-848-0310) to order using VISA or MasterCard, or for further information on books from Career Press.

The Career Press, Inc., 3 Tice Road, PO Box 687, Franklin Lakes, NJ 07417
www.careerpress.com
www.newpagebooks.com

Library of Congress Cataloging-in-Publication Data

Stewart, R. J., 1949-
The miracle tree : demystifying the Qabalah / by R.J. Stewart.
p. cm.
Includes bibliographical references and index.
ISBN 1-56414-650-2 (pbk.)
1. Cabala. I. Title.
BF1623.C2 S74 2003
135'.47—dc21   2002038686

Dedication

This book is dedicated to my friend and source of inspiration, Gareth Knight, one of the leading Western Qabalists of our time.

—R. J. Stewart

Contents

Foreword

How to use this book

In writing this book, my aim was to create a "reader-friendly" text, but not one that treats the reader as if he or she has no intelligence. Almost all spiritual or transformative traditions are oral and experiential rather than merely written: they often depend upon being there, rather than reading about being there. This poses some interesting tasks for the writer, who should write just as he or she would speak to a group of friends. When we talk as friends, we do not aim for the least intelligent level of communication, but for something that works equally for us all. In Qabalah, that *something* **is always the practical work in which we experience the Tree of Life directly. So this book offers a wealth of practical methods that you can use for your inner transformation through the Miracle Tree.**

First, I would recommend that you read through the entire book, like a novel, from beginning to end. Read it slowly, without haste, and do not rush into the practical work at first, until you have read the entire book. I know very well that everyone wants to try the exercises in a rush. This is a feature of our modern way of living. If you absolutely must have instant Qabalah, work with the first exercise in the book, the Rising Light, during the time you are reading through each chapter. But hold off on the rest until you have read the book…it will be worth the wait.

One of the better-known techniques of magical and spiritual work is to follow ideas in your sleep: many instructional and inspirational books (regardless of subject) may be read at bedtime, and when you do so, you should form a clear intention that you will pursue further understanding in your sleep. With *The Miracle Tree* you can begin this process immediately, as soon as you begin to read through the chapters.

The aim of this book is to demystify Qabalah, and to present ways of working with the Tree of Life in a direct manner, ways that you can prove for yourself. Qabalah is not the unique property of any religion or culture, but is a collection of traditions: such traditions are cultural, spiritual, and magical. So some parts of this book aim to clarify what these traditions may be, where they came from, and to explore the connections between different Qabalistic schools. This is not, however, a historical or literary research project. The origins of Qabalistic traditions, and their continuing use right up to the present day, form part of the background and foundation for practical work with the Miracle Tree, but they are not the Tree itself. Shocking as it may be to the literary historian, or the dogmatically inclined Qabalist, the texts of such traditions have no intrinsic value other than as curiosities if we fail to *practice* the material in our daily lives.

The language of this book is contemporary: it does not revert to terminology or alphabets that may be obscure to the reader. The most powerful spiritual language that we have is the language we learned as infants, for this is rooted deeply in the foundations of our consciousness. Thus no one language is more "sacred" than another, and all languages are equally sacred, for they all come from the primal urge to communicate.

We live in a time when many old patterns are disrupted, and new patterns are appearing. The Qabalah is not exempt from such powerful forces of change, and much of the Victorian, 19th, and early 20th centuries, literature on the subject, often the only literature for the European or American or English speaking reader, is hopelessly confused, and, more significant for us today, is socially and culturally outmoded.

So use this book to explore Qabalah afresh, and, when you have done the practical work, it will help you gain insights into some of the classic literature on the subject. Experience is of greater value than commentary.

When you read through the following chapters for the first time, you will discover that this book contains many practical ideas, exercises, and *forms*. Forms are concentrated simple ways of working with the Tree of Life. Do not be deceived, however, for this is not (yet another) "beginners guide." The forms have a curious property; they work equally for the beginner and for the experienced Qabalist. Wherever you are upon your Path, these forms will work powerfully for you. Rather than take my word for it, try them with an open mind for a few weeks of regular practice. Discover their effects for yourself, if you are an experienced Qabalist, or if you are only beginning your adventure with the Tree of Life.

Practical work

Once you have read the book from cover to cover (including the Appendices), begin to work through it, chapter by chapter. Try each form in turn: they are arranged in an order that is designed to lead us deeper into our spiritual experiences of the Tree of Life. Some of the early forms and essential Tree of Life meditations build a firm foundation for those more complex forms that appear in the later chapters. Some forms can stand alone; others go through successive stages of development. There is enough material in this book to last a lifetime: work with the initial forms, and then begin to develop the longer forms that develop through several stages.

If you want to systematize your work program, there are some simple patterns and schedules suggested in Appendix A. Or you can build your own, based on your experiences as you explore the forms, and build your awareness of the Tree of Life. You will find inspiration and understanding of your own rhythm for work with the Tree.

Once you have practiced the forms, and have gained familiarity with some of them, you should read the book straight through again. When you undertake this second reading, after you have trained in some of the forms, the book will seem very different, and you will discover many "hidden" aspects to the text. This revelatory quality is one of the features of Qabalah: many things can be said simultaneously through the language of the Tree of Life. This language is not English, Hebrew, Greek, Latin, or any specific language from any one land or race. It is the deeper language of living consciousness, which is at the foundation of all tongues, that which generates all words in this world and all worlds in the universe. Only when we are attuned to the Tree, do we discover some of the levels of meaning in any Qabalistic text, be it ancient or modern. Once you have practiced Qabalah, and have truly undertaken some of the practical work, you will always recognize the difference between a text that has been written by someone who practices, and one assembled by someone merely copying from other books to generate a product.

I would urge you to use this book steadily, rhythmically, stage by stage, but do not be tied or obsessed with small details. Qabalah works by holisms rather than by summary or analysis of its component parts, and Qabalistic literature has often suffered because of its neo-scientific emphasis upon details and parts that neglects the whole. This is why you should read the book through entirely, before practicing the forms, then read it again after some practice of each form. Upon the Tree of Life, the whole is always more than the sum of the parts.

The Tree of Life has revealed many miracles to Qabalists over millenniums. It has certainly done so for me, in my own life. I wish you peace and illumination in your exploration of *The Miracle Tree.*

—R. J. Stewart

Introduction

What is the Tree of Life?

This book has grown gradually out of seminars and workshops given in the United States and Britain, begun at a time before Qabalah suddenly became popular, but continuing into the present (early 21st century) when people are showing new interest in spiritual traditions associated with the Tree of Life. It is based on teaching and sharing with people, and on communicating my own years of experience of the Tree to others. For several centuries, only a few dedicated seekers have undertaken spiritual work with the Tree of Life. Today it is better known, due to the upsurge of interest in spiritual, personal, and inner transformation. Our first question in a class, group, or book should be: *What is the Tree of Life?* Even those with experience of Qabalah may benefit from considering this question afresh. The answers are astonishing. Many people study Qabalah without asking what, in truth, is the Tree of Life?

We are the Tree of Life

The Tree is not a picture in a book, not a set of symbols, not a system of meditation and vision, though it is frequently described as such. It is not even a tradition, though there are several traditions that work with the Tree (these are outlined later). To discover the Tree of Life, we should discover simple, direct ways of experiencing our own Being. Nothing more, nothing less.

We are already the Tree of Life. We do not have to study it, learn obscure phrases, or wrestle with confusing texts. It is a Tree of Life, not a Tree of Literature; it is a Tree of Wonders, not a Tree of Words. It is a Miracle Tree, for when we work with it directly, it makes profound changes within us, in our lives. When miracles happen, we are changed forever. The miracle of the Tree of Life is that it changes us from a false and imbalanced state to our real and eternal Being.

In the following chapters, much of the material you might find in a typical book on Qabalah and the Tree of Life does not appear. Why should it? There are many books all restating the same checklists and phrases. This is not one of them. What you will find here are ways of participation and experience, working directly with the Tree of Life, to bring transformation and change. Many of these methods have not been published before, and are unique to this book. They have been tried and tested over the years, and until now have only been taught privately to small groups of students.

Meeting people in seminars or workshops, one question that I hear over and over, in various forms, is: "Why is Qabalah so complex?" The answer that I always give is: *Qabalah is not complex, but is simple and direct.*

Much of the published Qabalistic literature, dating from the 19th century to the present day, is, however, stunningly complex. This literature is not, in itself, Qabalah, and it is certainly not the Tree of Life. Because one particular genre of writing about a subject is confused, sometimes incoherent, and often incomprehensible, does not nullify the subject itself. This is especially true when we consider books on Qabalah and the Tree of Life.

Suppose there were no books?

Rather than discuss the comparative flaws and benefits of standard books on Qabalah, we can sidestep this issue, and cut directly to the chase. How would we approach the Tree of Life without books? For some people, this is a daunting question, as there is kind of glamour in complexity of words and obsessive obscurity of texts. Yet the early Qabalists, who were explorers of the spiritual worlds, had no books. Everything was experienced directly and kept in living memory. What happened? Why can we not do as they did?

The answer is that as their material was gradually written down, and later found its way into publication, texts replaced experience. Of course we can do what the early Qabalists did, and more, for there is nothing to stop us. The problem is not with books, but with what books on the Tree of Life have become in modern literature. Once you have a published text about a spiritual method, people who have not experienced or practiced the method can copy it. This is frequently the case with books on Qabalah, rather like mistaking a much-copied map for a real journey.

We sometimes forget, or overlook, the fact that living Qabalah and experiencing the Tree of Life relies upon oral traditions that were never written down. This is not through elitism or selfish secrecy, but because much of the material has to be experienced and shared, rather than merely described in textbook form.

I would argue, strongly, that due to changes in culture, and changes in human consciousness, we might now share some of the primary "secret" techniques through direct teaching, and communicate them through a new kind of book. That is this book, which comes as close as possible to the way I would teach if we were sitting in a group together, experiencing the Tree of Life. Some aspects of oral teaching cannot be reproduced in print: there are subtle energies of communication and participation that may only be shared "live." However, there are ways of opening these subtle energies that can be adapted to print, provided you, the reader, are willing to work with them in your spiritual practices and daily life. There are no secrets; there are only varied ways of sharing reality and truth.

This is a book that will show you how to work without books. You will not have to look in the index for a color or a Hebrew, Latin, or Greek word before you meditate, and eventually you will not need the book at all. This is a book about how to experience the Tree of Life directly.

Clear away the clutter: Discover where you are

Suppose you were someone who had never read a book, never meditated. Not an ignorant person, but an innocent one: as indeed we all are within, for we are all aspects of the primal Eve/Adam, the androgynous being that is central to Qabalistic transformation upon the Tree of Life. As an innocent or primal human you would see, sense, feel, and know that there are certain inherent patterns to life on Earth. Picture yourself: the primal human (no cell phone, laptop, or PDA). You stand with your feet upon the Earth, your head toward the sky. Above you, at certain times, is the Moon, then the Sun, then the Stars. *Earth, Moon, Sun, Stars*.

Like a tree, with its roots in the Earth, our understanding, our relative sense of place, grows from the ground toward the Stars. This quality of *relatedness* within us, all about us, is the Tree of Life. *We are already the Tree of Life; indeed, we do not, and could not, exist without it.*

Reach for the Stars

The simplicity of being aware of Earth, Moon, Sun, and Stars is both the beginning and the most advanced stage of working with the Tree of Life. There is nothing else, for it is everything. To reach for the Stars we do not need symbols, attributes, words, names, letters, colors, rays, planes and subplanes, or any of the accumulated lists found in most books. We just need to reach, as a tree reaches. Earth, Moon, Sun, and Stars are already within us, and we exist already within them. This is not an obscure proposition but a physical fact. The practice of Qabalah, and associated experiences of the powers of the Tree of Life, is, and has always been, physical, and not merely mental, textual, or abstract. Nor has it ever been "spiritual" in an escapist manner. We are made of the stuff of Earth, around which orbits the Moon. Moon and Earth are part of the Solar System, which is part of the universe of Stars. We could only be separate from this reality in the false separation of materialist culture, where our eyes are kept firmly upon the freeway and the stock market, sometimes for good reasons, but too often without seeing anything else.

Remember your roots

The Tree of Life is exactly what it is, a tree. It was not by error or through simplistic ignorance that the early

Qabalists showed spiritual transformation through the emblem of a tree. All trees have roots: without them a tree will not grow. If a tree is cut off from its roots, it topples over and dies. We might also remember this; that a sapling exposed to too much light from above, without a strong root system, will spring up quickly, but then wither and die. Such simple truths have been utterly forgotten, or ignored, even suppressed, in literature on the Tree of Life. The roots of the Tree of Life, for us in this world, are deep in our sacred Planet Earth. Thus our spiritual work with the Tree should begin where it germinates, where it finds a major part of its nourishment, in the fruitful Earth. This is both the land in which you live, and our Planet Earth upon and within which we all live.

We live in a culture that ignores, exploits, and destroys the Earth. Working with the Miracle Tree is both transformative and redemptive for us, provided we are aware of the roots, and learn how to use them in our spiritual work. In the major theme of Earth awareness, this book is different from Qabalistic literature in general, which ignores or repudiates roots as being "evil." Why are the roots of the Tree of Life evil? Are the roots of an oak tree or of a flower evil? No…and neither are the roots of the world tree, the Miracle Tree.

The Sacred UnderWorld

In ancestral cultures, the realms beneath the surface of the Earth were regarded with reverence, but it is not so today. Far from sensing a spiritual dimension to the Earth and oceans, we use them as dumping grounds for poisonous waste and radioactive materials. The idea that the UnderWorld, the realm into which all roots reach, is "evil" is inherited from a naïve dualistic worldview, the product of political religion. This same worldview, somewhat transformed, but still rejecting the sanctity of the Planet, has created the materialism that destroys and pollutes even as you read these words. Nothing helps us more with our awakening from antagonistic dualism than the flow of the Tree of Life: a flow, a movement, a rhythm that links Earth, Moon, Sun, and Stars, through the human body.

Most Qabalistic practices consist of remembering who, what, and where we are, and, beyond this process of remembering, increasing our participation and presence in the living universe, the Being of which our *being* is an inherent part.

Practical Work with the Tree of Life: Qabalistic Forms

Our practical work begins in Chapter 1. Much of this book emphasizes and explores what you can actually do through working with the Tree of Life, rather than merely listing or describing its attributes. Most of the practical work in the following chapters is described through sets of *forms*. Forms (found in martial arts, and in traditional music, poetry, and Wisdom teachings worldwide) are units of practice that may be combined together in flowing patterns of interaction. They gradually replace the standard ideas of ceremonies, meditations, visualizations, and so forth. The forms in this book have a progression, a flow whereby they enhance one another increasingly as you work with them. *Forms* may be visual, physical, meditative, active, passive, or any of those. They may be ceremonial or mystical, visible or invisible. By using forms, we cut across many of the false categories and divisive analyses of spiritual practice. A form is a form: it works through the interaction of body and spirit. All forms are simple, direct, and practical.

Unlike most texts on the Tree, which begin in the heavens, we begin where a tree finds its nourishment, in the roots. The first forms that we work with bring us into a strong relationship with the nourishing roots of the Tree of Life, and from this firm foundation, we can ascend to the Stars.

If you wish, you may go straight to Chapter 1 now. If you want a short summary of the background of the Qabalistic traditions, which I would recommend as part of your attunement to the spiritual practices themselves, please read on.

The Three Streams of Qabalah

This section is not, strictly speaking, essential for your practical work with the Tree of Life. However, many people in classes and workshops have found that a short, basic history is helpful, as it clarifies some of the typical misunderstandings of Qabalistic tradition that are rife in publication.

What is Qabalah? The word simply means an oral teaching, or whispered Wisdom, mouth to ear. Thus we should really speak of *Qabalahs*, plural. Any coherent tradition of oral Wisdom, handed on by word of mouth, is Qabalah. There are several major Qabalahs, or streams of Qabalah. The word itself is Hebrew, and is now so widely used that it would be pointless to try to coin another term, especially as one of the major streams of Qabalah is Jewish. Qabalah also means sharing spiritual experience: the original early texts were merely skeletal notes, and the verbal teaching and shared experience was the true exposition of the Tree of Life. Regrettably the word Qabalah has come to be used as something furtive, selfishly secretive, or conspiratorial, yet it has nothing to do with covert groups, plots, or hidden secrets. Indeed, the secrets of the

Tree of Life are wide open: we just need to be reminded how to experience them.

The First Stream of Qabalah

At present the most popular form of Qabalah in Western modernist culture is a simplified variant of Jewish tradition. This has become fashionable with film stars and famous personalities, and has a vigorous outreach program beyond Judaism. Nevertheless, it has its roots in a venerable esoteric tradition long practiced within Judaism, though not always with orthodox approval. This popular form arises out of the first of the Three Streams of Jewish Qabalah, but is not truly representative of enduring Jewish mysticism, as it has been modified for a more general non-Jewish audience. Thus it has some aspects of Hebrew mystical tradition, but many of the practices have been adjusted and simplified.

There are several schools of Jewish Qabalah (in the sense of enduring lines of teaching through the centuries), traceable to revered individual teachers, either historical or legendary. Jewish Qabalah uses the sacred letters of the Hebrew alphabet, and the mystical combinations of words, letters, and numbers, from sacred texts. Some Jewish Qabalists use the Tree of Life, in the graphic forms that are familiar to most people (*see figure 1, pg.33*), while others do not. The graphic Tree is not central to Jewish Qabalah, though it is often assumed to be so by non-Jewish writers. To truly partake of this tradition, you must be Jewish, speak Hebrew, and live within the traditional contextual world of Judaism. Very few non-Jewish people can achieve such cultural assimilation. Many contemporary Qabalists borrow freely, yet fragmentally, from Jewish tradition, but will not truly enter into it.

There are centuries of deep spiritual art and discipline in Jewish Qabalah, and it rightly demands a total commitment and a presence in Jewish culture and tradition. Only then are its deepest secrets revealed, through changes of consciousness and energy within the Qabalist. Jewish Qabalah is said, traditionally, to have come from the patriarch Abraham, who received it from a mysterious spiritual source. The same is said of the second stream of Qabalah, that of Sufi mysticism within Islam. Both, therefore, imply that they came from some older source. This source, "Abraham," is essentially *ancestral Wisdom*, but it also has a historical origin hidden in the mists of time.

The authoritative scholar of Jewish tradition, Gerschom Scholem[1], concludes that Qabalah came in to Jewish culture from sources in ancient Persia: the same conclusion was reached by an Adolphe Franck[2], an eminent French Jewish scholar in the 19th century. This historical transmission helps us to understand that the traditions of Qabalah are ancient, passed down through the ages, through differing races and cultures, with certain enduring aspects. Qabalah and the Tree of Life are not "owned" by any one culture, race, or religion.

This is true for one simple reason: Qabalah describes *that which is present*, the nature of Being, and reveals ways of relating to life at all levels. Though there are cultural expressions of Qabalah, such as the three streams we are outlining here, and others, the true or "inner" tradition is both pan-cultural and transcultural.

The Second Stream of Qabalah

The second stream, Sufi Qabalah, is now found within the context of mystical Islam. Sufis often imply that their traditions and practices predate orthodox Islam, just as Hebrew Qabalah predates orthodox Judaism.

The relationship between these two streams is found at a very deep level, rather than within the orthodox host religions themselves. Both use certain visionary techniques, commune with angelic consciousness, and both revere the forbidden Feminine in spiritual practices. Sufi mysticism has a practical branch that works with *jinn,* the spirit beings of the land and Planet. We will return to this idea shortly, when we summarize the third stream.

Both Jewish Qabalah and Sufi Qabalah have an uneasy relationship with orthodox religion, yet both have endured for centuries. The Tree of Life is found in various forms within both; how could it not be so? The Tree is the reality of the Earth, Moon, Sun, and Stars, so it will be present, and is present, in many spiritual traditions worldwide. Indeed, the miracle of the Tree is that it embodies a perennial flow of traditions, all describing the reality of our being upon Earth. As such, it both transcends, and acts as a foundation for, all formal religions and magical or spiritual arts.

Each of the two streams described, Jewish and Sufi, also places considerable emphasis upon the spiritual lineage of holy teachers, saints, and sometimes legendary or mythical mentors. Indeed, you would not be able to practice either Sufi or Jewish Qabalah without being initiated within one or more of these highly individual lineages. Such connections are more than historical or cultural. The living consciousness of the mentors is intentionally sought, as a source, as a spiritual presence, that enlivens the Qabalah, and guides the seeker upon the Tree of Life.

The Golden Age of Qabalah in Spain

Jewish and Arabic cultures exchanged knowledge freely during the Middle Ages in Spain, at a time when many of the older Qabalistic texts were first written out, having been previously preserved in memory alone. At this time they also came into contact with the third stream, that of Western tradition. It is this stream that we work with, so I will give this a little more space and explanation, bearing in mind that there was much interaction between all three during the Middle Ages.

The Third Stream of Qabalah

The Western Tradition of Qabalah, the Tree of Life, and related spiritual practices, all have a rather confused history, often repeated in publication, and frequently reported incorrectly. It is generally assumed that the Western stream borrowed extensively from Jewish and Islamic mysticism in the Middle Ages, and took the practices into a broadly Christian, but heretical and forbidden, framework. This is true of Christian Qabalah, but is not true of the tradition itself.

Just as Jewish and Arabic mysticism inherited older traditions of Qabalah and the Tree of Life, so did the mysticism and magical arts of "the West," by which we mean the North and West; or the innate ancestral sacro-magical traditions of Europe, the Mediterranean, and many adjoining regions. We should not fall into the propaganda trap, so often stated, that the West has no spirituality of its own. This is only true as far as bankrupt formal religion and materialism is concerned. In fact, the West has vast and often untapped spiritual riches, which we can easily discover. These spiritual riches are within a treasure house hidden in full view.

One of the best documented sources is the philosophy of the ancient Greeks: Western Qabalah is often called Neo-Platonic Qabalah for this reason, or Hermetic Qabalah, as the mythical mentor of the tradition was Hermes, the god of thought and communication. Texts reputedly by Hermes Trismegistos (Thrice Great) form one of several foundation stones for Western Qabalah.

The geometric or mathematical patterns of the Tree of Life (*figure 1, pg. 33*) are essentially derived from the philosophy and metaphysics known to Plato, Pythagoras, and other ancient Greek exponents. The numerical, musical, geometric, and abstract metaphysical patterns described by these ancient philosophers were not devised by them, but were statements of extant traditions that they sought to expound and develop.

The geometric form of the Tree of Life was incorporated, occasionally, into both Jewish and Sufi Qabalah during and after the Middle Ages, and eventually became thought of as "standard." In truth, there are many ways of drawing a Tree of Life, and some of them are explored in our chapters on practical work with the Tree. Modern writers often become hopelessly entangled in pseudo-scientific or psychological explanations of ancient metaphysics and sacred mathematics or sacred geometry: while this may be interesting intellectually, and can occasionally be inspiring, it means nothing whatsoever without the Living Spiritual experience of the Tree of Life.

As noted earlier, it is often stated with false authority that a fusion of Jewish, Islamic, and Greek philosophy in Spain during the Middle Ages gave rise to Western Qabalah. This is partly true, as far as some early texts are concerned, but it is far too simplistic and is based on lack of research.

The Tree of Life, in various forms, was known to Celtic, Teutonic, and Norse traditions, and to Mediterranean and Eastern European ancestral cultures. Some of these traditions gradually passed into Wisdom traditions embodied in the oral poetry and in the mystical imagery of medieval Europe, and this poetic imagery is the broad foundation of Western Qabalah. Not only broad, but also ancient, with sources in the remote ancestral past. Just as the Hebrew Qabalah has its threshold texts from the Middle Ages, and the Sufi Qabalah has its great medieval poets, so does the Western Qabalah have undeniable early source texts. We will come to some of these shortly.

The Third Stream and the Sacred Land

Included within the Third Stream, or western tradition of Qabalah, is the idea of working with the spirits of the land, a concept that is found also in Sufi Qabalah with traditions concerning the *jinn*, and which later forms a major part of Renaissance magic. In the Northern or European context, these are the faery beings that occupy the forests, streams, mountains, rivers, and seas. Interaction with them is the basis of all folkloric magic, and was absorbed into the so-called secret aspects of Qabalah. When the 16th century mystical Rosicrucian texts began to appear, they proposed a type of Qabalistic mysticism that involved working with the spiritual forces of the sacred mountains and the underworld: a theme well known in folkloric faery tradition. Today we would call it *environmental magic*, and it should form a major part of any new approach to spiritual awareness and transformation.

Many writers, failing to do their homework, have assumed that there are no early western texts that present a Qabalistic tradition, other than those that came out of the golden age of cultural exchange in medieval Spain. This is simply untrue: much of the western tradition can be found within, and profitably compared to, two major source texts that have been ignored or neglected.

The 12th century Merlin texts

Two major texts from the 12th century, unknown to Victorian occultists, and ignored in modern books on Qabalah (as they mainly copy 19th century sources), are the *Prophecies* and *Life of Merlin*, set into Latin by Geoffrey of Monmouth. They are adaptations and developments of poetic lore, from the oral traditions of the Welsh bards. Both have highly sophisticated elements of Qabalah, the Tree of Life, and related magic, philosophy and mysticism, deeply woven into their legendary texts. These are actual and historical texts, so their existence is not a debatable or theoretical proposition, and they are firmly identified and verified by scholars of medieval literature. Our interest, however, is in the spiritual, magical, and metaphysical material that runs through these texts, and this is substantial, coherent, and Qabalistic in nature.

As early as the 12th century, (around 1131 C.E.) there were long poems in Welsh or Breton, in which Merlin, as a boy, an adult, and an old man, was the central character. They formed part of the widespread oral poetic tradition, which was, at that time, being assembled and transcribed by various known and anonymous chroniclers: we could call this tradition "Celtic," but its themes are embedded in many European folk tales, poems, ballads, and songs. Please be aware that these poems are emphatically *not* about the wise-old-Merlin of popular fiction or of modern entertainment or fantasy, but describe a different Merlin, representing mystical insight and prophecy through initiation and interaction with both natural and supernatural forces.

In the early middle ages, the Irish legendary cycles, deriving from oral epic poetry, were preserved by monastic scribes, while the Welsh bardic poems and tales were likewise noted, and sometimes expanded upon, by contemporary commentators and historians. The Merlin legends are a major example of this process.

These "Merlin" sources contain cosmology, metaphysics, and an allegorical life cycle described as a set of dramatic and often perilous adventures leading from the world of

Earth to the Wisdom of the Stars. They are not influenced by, nor do they quote from, the standard Qabalistic source texts from medieval Spain; indeed, they predate such texts *(see the Bibliography)*.

The Merlin texts were transcribed from an oral, poetic, and prophetic tradition, circulated by traveling bards and poets in what we would nowadays call "Celtic" culture. They contain apocalyptic Prophecies, independent of, and substantially different from, the Christian Book of Revelation. They also contain Celtic and some ancient Greek elements, images, and characters, and have very little Christian content. The writer and chronicler Geoffrey of Monmouth reworked these bardic sources into polished Latin prose and poetry, and could, presumably, escape religious criticism, for he presented the stories as ancient British histories or legends, as entertainment with moral value, rather than as overtly mystical or spiritual allegories.

The material of the Merlin texts, as presented by Geoffrey, but deriving from an older oral tradition, is essentially Qabalistic, and relates directly to the Tree of Life. It was not devised or invented by Geoffrey, but was a synthesis of the widespread Celtic poetic and prophetic tradition of his mother's Welsh or Breton people, mixed with elements of the philosophy and metaphysics of the time. It differs in many ways from the medieval Christian worldview, and was presented as a thematic collection of entertaining Wisdom tales and poems, not to be confused with formal religion. This same method, by the way, is widely used in Sufi storytelling, in which humorous or elevating stories are told, songs are sung, and poems recited. Indeed, this method of teaching Wisdom and insight was found in all the older traditions worldwide.

There are two highly significant identifying aspects of this bardic Qabalah from the 12th century: the first is that it features a goddess, repeatedly, as a major figure. In the Merlin texts she is called Ariadne, the Weaver goddess. The second is that the texts describe, vividly and specifically, encapsulated sets of images and persons, and offer detailed descriptions of their interaction in a spiritual drama. These are the earliest known descriptions of what would later become tarot trumps in Renaissance Italy. They are found in the Merlin texts some 300 years before the first hand painted tarot cards, and offer many insights into the origins of tarot in poetic oral tradition in Europe, origins as *forms* or images, characters, and themes, that interact with one another and can be assembled to create Wisdom stories.

We will refer to these source texts from time to time, as some of our practical work is derived from ideas and images within them.

Conclusion

When you work with the forms in this book, when you explore the Tree of Life, you are working within a well established and enduring spiritual tradition, with several major branches. Our presentation and practices are essentially Western, but they are not contemporary devices, so much as creative and original variants of perennial techniques and concepts. They embody an ancient tradition that can be traced at least as early as the 12th century, and that 12th century threshold period marks the transition of the material from oral to written sources. But just as in Jewish or Sufi Qabalah, which were embodied at around the same time, the written sources from the medieval period did not replace or block the ongoing oral and inner teachings. Such teachings continued for long after the first written reports or transcriptions of oral Wisdom tales, poems, and visions.

Let us proceed now to our practical work with the Miracle Tree, exploring the concepts and practices of the Tree of Life, demystifying Qabalah.

Illustrations

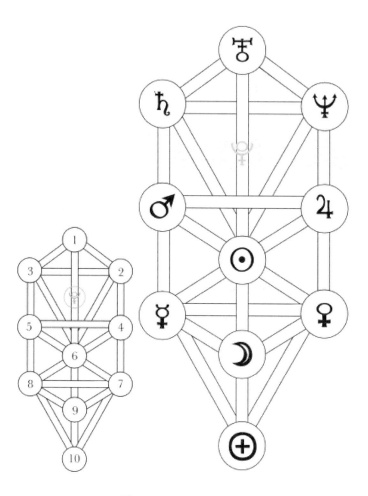

Figure 1. Tree of Life

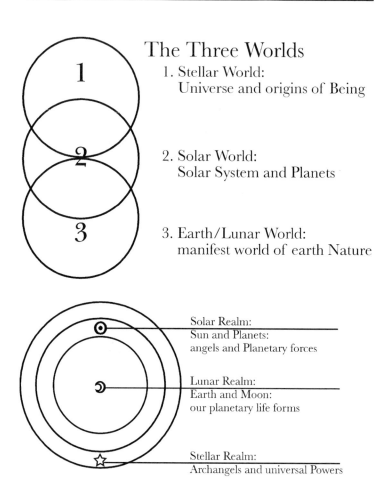

The Three Worlds

1. Stellar World:
   Universe and origins of Being

2. Solar World:
   Solar System and Planets

3. Earth/Lunar World:
   manifest world of earth Nature

Solar Realm:
Sun and Planets:
angels and Planetary forces

Lunar Realm:
Earth and Moon:
our planetary life forms

Stellar Realm:
Archangels and universal Powers

Figure 2. Three Worlds

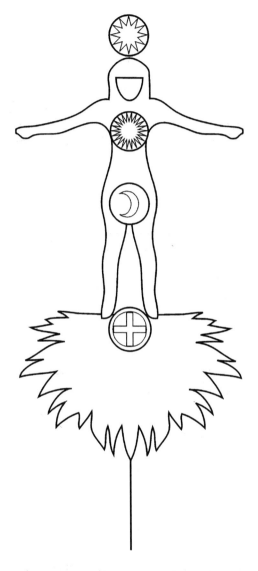

Figure 3. Rising Light

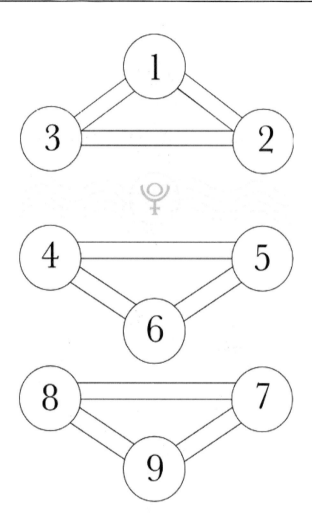

Figure 4. Lunar, Solar, and Stellar Triads

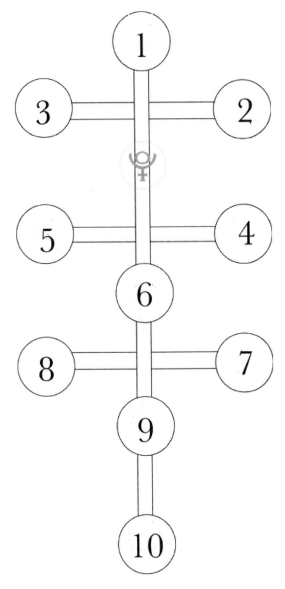

Figure 5. Three Wheels

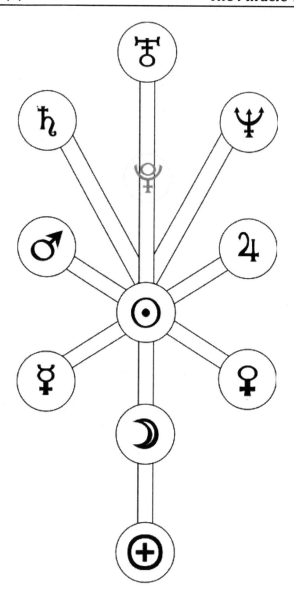

Figure 6. Radiant Paths

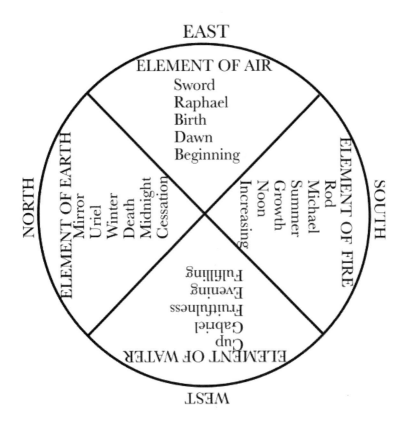

Figure 7. Universal Map

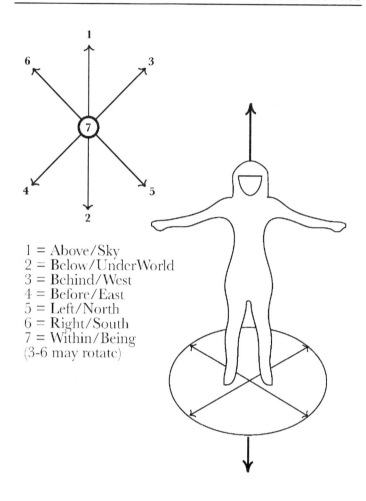

1 = Above/Sky
2 = Below/UnderWorld
3 = Behind/West
4 = Before/East
5 = Left/North
6 = Right/South
7 = Within/Being
(3-6 may rotate)

Figure 8. Seven Directions

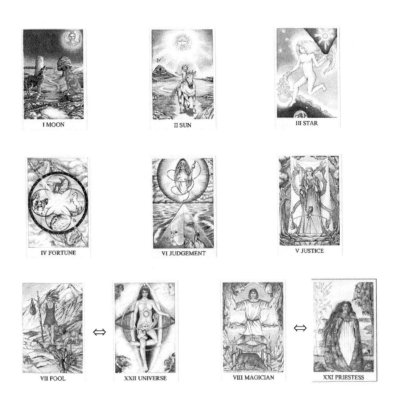

Figure 9. Path Images (1)

Figure 10. Path Images (2)

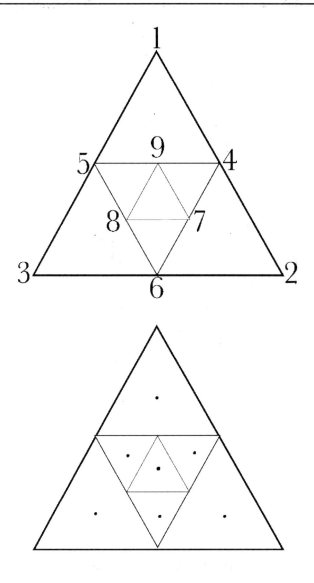

Figure 11. Alternative Tree of Life

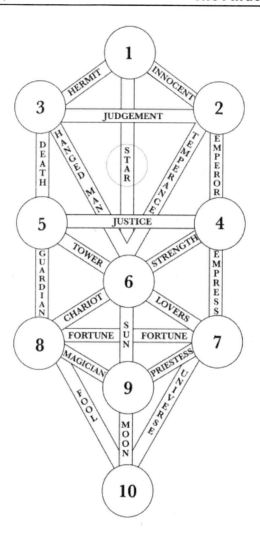

Figure 12. Paths on Tree

Chapter 1

Working with Forms

The Tree of Life, Ritual Magic, and Mysticism

Qabalah is often divided into two categories in literature, Practical and Theoretical. The Practical involves, we are advised, the use of Ritual Magic, ceremonial invocation of powers and Beings, and outward focused intent. The Theoretical, it is said, involves meditation, visualization, and inward seeking intent. In modern practice, the Theoretical has tended to lean towards intellectual comparisons and speculations, often moving away from the inner practices. At least, that is the gist of most literature from the 19th century onwards. Early Qabalistic teachings and associated texts, prior to the Victorian era, often give dire warnings against practical Qabalah. Learn all the symbols, names of angels, sacred letters, and their associated powers, but never do anything practical with them. In some texts, prohibition against invocation is included.

Such prohibitions are found in traditional Jewish Qabalah, and from there have spilled over into Christian Qabalah. Thus Athanasius Kircher, the 17th century Jesuit polymath, could set out tables of angels, powers, Planets, metals, and spiritual forces, but qualified with the well-established prohibition against using them for anything. The politics of Christianity play a strong role, of course, but the idea of two categories of Qabalah, Practical and Theoretical, seem to precede dogmatic correctness, in both Jewish and Christian traditions: and the dualism runs through the majority of "occult" and esoteric texts on Qabalah. So we have the impression of a divided set of applications: the Practical, which no one wants you to undertake, and the Theoretical, which must never spill over into practice.

The modern individual could be confused, even misled, by this pattern that runs through Qabalistic literature. Clearly much of the division is propaganda, and not merely religious dogmatic propaganda. If something comes to you with an admonition..."Never do this...read about it...but never do it. See this map? Study it, but never go there, it is bad for you..." what is your response? There is more to this situation than meets the eye. In the long history of the war between dictatorial religion and independent spiritual traditions there is a gray zone, somewhere between the two factions. When we are told, by authority, that something is bad or evil, and by the esoteric traditions that it is inadvisable or dangerous, then that something is usually powerful. No one wants you to do it, be it, or think it. You might acquire independence!

There is a simple way to bypass this stagnant backwater: the division between Practical Qabalah and Theoretical Qabalah is not only contrived and false, but also utterly impossible to implement in practice. The Practical Qabalah is really the Magical Qabalah, using magical arts to transform your relationship with the Tree of Life. The Theoretical Qabalah is really the Mystical Qabalah, using techniques of vision and contemplation to comprehend the Tree of Life. From this point on, let us think in terms of Magical and Mystical, rather ran Practical and Theoretical. As soon as we do this, many of the false divisions fade away. Consider this simple truth: *You cannot practice ritual magic without a mystical content: you cannot be a mystic without conducting magical rituals*. Not, of course, the romantic notion of reading occult rituals from a big book, while dressed up and engaging in grandiose wand-waving, but something else altogether: living a life of ritual pattern-making. This can include formal ceremonies, or can be as simple as meditations while walking or silent withdrawn contemplation. They are all practical, all magical, and all mystical. Any intentional action is a magical ritual, especially if the intent is towards spiritual transformation and altered awareness.

All spiritual forces flow into, and out of, the human body. As soon as we undertake a focused action, an intention with spiritual associations, we are engaged in both Magical and Mystical Qabalah, in both ceremony and mysticism simultaneously. While we can say that some ways of working are less obviously formal, and some are more obviously formal, we cannot truly separate magic and mysticism.

The popular trappings of ritual magic, as we all know nowadays, are mainly dross and fantasy, yet there is a basic core of practical magic that has enduring concepts worldwide, in all spiritual traditions. It is often called the perennial tradition, but is not so much a tradition, as a set of provocative statements about the nature of being alive on Planet Earth. Provocative because these statements challenge our rigid conditioned preconceptions, and encourage us to think and explore for ourselves. This perennial Wisdom finds its place in Magical (practical) Qabalah, and is immensely useful to us in our work with the Tree of Life.

In this book, we approach the Miracle Tree through forms. Some forms are more ceremonial and outward focused; others are more contemplative and inwardly focused. They represent nothing more or less than the tidal flow of spiritual forces into and out of the human body. Providing we use this idea as our ground, there is no false division between Magical and Mystical. The Magical tends to flow from within to without; the Mystical tends to flow from without to within. But, like all tides, one cannot exist without the other, and the Foundation of Life (the 9th Emanation of Being, or 9th sphere on the Tree, embodied for us by the Moon) draws all tides equally in sequence.

After more than 30 years of practicing Qabalah, it occurred to me that the divisions found in literature are meaningless. They represent either suppressive propaganda "don't do it…because we do it and we don't want you to learn about it," or a dualism generated by cultural perspectives "are you a practical type, or a mystical type?" The answer to this second question is that it does not matter, as Tree of Life disciplines and the spiritual forces associated with them, make no such division. Where such divisions exist, work with the Tree dissolves them, and all such bindings are loosed.

However, cultural stereotypes run deep, so we find that much in publication, especially from the short-lived but influential psychological fashions of the 20th century, will follow this dualistic perspective of practical and theoretical, active and passive, magical and mystical, and so forth. Thus a divided world is perpetuated by the very methods that were originally conceived to unite it.

This may seem like a small matter of contention, but from a magical perspective, it is deeply significant. Once an individual is told, by acceptable authority "you are X," one will usually follow the Path of X. Indeed, we become X because we have been told that we are it, whatever category or analytical type it may be. So beware of deciding if you are magician or a mystic...you are always both, and many combinations thereof.

The Miracle Tree liberates us from stereotypes. We are no more bound to a fixed pattern in our lives than the weather is bound to the hours of the clock. Yes, there are patterns within us, but they are many, and interwoven with one another. This is shown on the Tree of Life, and we can free ourselves from restrictive and repetitive patterns by working with the Tree. This is indeed miraculous to someone trapped in the conditioned world, but gradually becomes central to the life of the Qabalist.

The Lunar Triad (*see figure 4, pg. 36*) is where most of our conditioned patterns occur, and the Tree is especially helpful because it reveals that such patterns can be transformed by working with the Solar or Stellar Triads. If you work with a rooted Tree, as we do in this book, you can also untangle aspects of the personality through the Roots of the Tree. This UnderWorld aspect of Qabalah is the equivalent of the Shortened Way found in many spiritual traditions worldwide. And of course, there are many prohibitions against it. So many, that modern Tree of Life books and classes work with a rootless tree. A rootless tree! No wonder we destroy the life-giving rain forests for short-term profit. That which is found in the spiritual traditions, even the most obscure, will manifest into the outer world.

The Rising Light Form

The benefit of forms is that they cross over between the false boundaries of magical and mystical, practical and theoretical. The roots of the Tree are in the Planet, the land, and the oceans. They are in the vital forces that arise in the human body from beneath the feet. So in Tree of Life work with groups, we often begin with a form that attunes us to this flow of vital forces.

The Rising Light Below

This is a simple but powerful form for arousing energy and passing it through your body. The power that rises from the UnderWorld, the Light within the Earth, will awaken and transform your own energies far more effectively than concentrating in isolation upon your power centers or chakras. It is the human equivalent of the Tree of Life, drawing power up through the roots. If you do this exercise once every day, you will realign and activate your inner or subtle energies, and gain greater vitality. It will prepare you for the other forms or methods of working with the Tree that are described later.

The Rising Light Below exercise is most effective while standing, though it may also be done sitting cross-legged, as squatting and cross-legged postures enhance our Earth contact. Here are the stages, with some brief notes:

1. Begin with a period of silence and steady breathing. Your arms are lowered, with the fingertips stretched and pointing towards the ground. If you are sitting they may touch the ground lightly or rest upon your thighs. This initial arm position is important, as you will be raising your arms gradually.

2. Feel the point of contact between your body and the ground. If this is the floor of a room, feel that the building is in contact with the ground, with the land.

This exercise is enhanced by working directly upon the surface of the land, or in a cave, basement, or underground chamber. By the holism, paradox, or "Law" of reflections and octaves, it also works very well in high places, such as the tops of mountains, hills, and in tall buildings.

Many UnderWorld or Earth Light techniques are useful for those of us who live in a city environment, as they pass directly through the imbalanced enervating city energy field, which has little or no effect upon them. If you live in an unhealthy, energy-isolated building, do this exercise on the roof or in the basement as well as in your own apartment.

3. Visualize a source of energy just below the ground or floor where your feet or body make contact. This is often felt and seen as a flowing or pulsing ball of Light. The upper surface of this energy sphere touches the soles of your feet (or your legs and body if you are sitting in a cross-legged position) and from its lower surface, a strand of Light descends into the heart of the land, into the depths of the planetary heart. This is your root structure, your reflected energy field in the UnderWorld, normally latent. You are going to activate it, bring it alive through conscious participation. Remember that it is already part of you, your rooted and reflected energy, which you do not normally access or use, something of which millions of people are completely unaware, even those who practice meditation and energy techniques.

4. Increase your awareness of this energy sphere: feel it touching you, move your imagination into it. You may feel your personal energies descending into it, and a sensation of heat where your body touches the ground.

5. Gradually draw the energy source into yourself. Do so by breathing steadily and feeling the
energy sphere rise through your feet into your
body. You arm/hand position is slowly raised,
drawing the energy with it. There are four zones
of the body/energy field: FEET/GENITALS/
HEART/HEAD *(see figure 3, pg. 35)*.

These zones are essential to practical Qabalah and Tree
of Life work. They are our human reflection of the Tree
of Life, the holism of the Elements and Worlds of Earth,
Moon, Sun, and Stars.

6. Feet: be aware of the Element of Earth, and
the matter or substance of your entire body.
The energy sphere rises up through your feet,
legs, and thighs. Your arms are still directed
downwards, but slowly rising upward, drawing the energy as they move.

7. Loins or Genitals: be aware of the Element
of Water, and the twofold nature of Water in
your body. Firstly it is the fundamental element of your cells; on a nonphysical level
Water is the element of creation, birth, sexual
union, love, and represents the second awakening of energy within your physical substance. Your arms are raised gradually to
waist height.

8. Heart: be aware of the Element of Fire. As
the energy sphere rises, it gradually becomes
more incandescent. The Four Elements are
simultaneously physical and metaphysical. At
this heart level, the increasing rate of your
energy becomes Fire. In your body this is bio-
electrical energy, the flow of blood, and the
subtle forces that radiate from your Life core.

As these subtle forces manifest, they appear in an increasingly watery and earthy form. The fiery incandescence of the energy sphere rising from the UnderWorld through your body is the third awakening of energy within your physical substance. Your arms are raised, palms upward, to shoulder height.

9. Throat: be aware of the Element of Air. The energy has now risen to surround your head and shoulders, and has reached its most rapid and mobile rate. All four zones are now alive, each rising through the body, merging within one another. Your arms are raised above the head, palms upward. Finally you bring the fingertips together, gently touching. Hold this position for a few moments.

10. Returning the power. Simply reverse the sequence by steadily lowering your arms and feeling the power pass down through your body. It returns steadily to your energy sphere within the land, below your feet. As it descends, you lower your arms, and each of the four zones gently reduces in activity.

This exercise is easy to do, and takes only two or three minutes to practice. I have been teaching this Earth Light or Roots form to people for about 17 years, with many beneficial results. It works because the Earth Light is present at the roots of the Tree of Life in our Planet. We only need to come into a better relationship, a more conscious participation, to benefit from its circulation.

The *Rising Light* form is a practice that frees us, and loosens many of the typical barriers that can block or inhibit other Tree of Life techniques. Try it once a day, for a few minutes. Once you have done this for a week or two, start working with the walking form, called *Walking Participation*, which is described shortly.

More About Forms

Most simple and powerful exercises in spiritual arts are similar in concept to those of martial arts: they are forms. We can use the term forms to describe any simple pattern or practice. With experience, we learn how to combine different patterns or forms, though in early practice, we do them one at a time. Using the idea of forms rather than meditations, visualizations or Path-workings, opens us to many potentials. While some forms are accessible through meditation or vision, and some are enhanced by such techniques, many of the forms that we learn from the Tree of Life are unique unto themselves, often working through the body. They are vehicles or modes, natural fusions of innate qualities of consciousness and energy that we all have latent within us. In this approach to Qabalah, the forms are central, and the popular idea of correspondences and symbols is regarded as a secondary practice, used only to supplement your practical work. So, in this book, a number of forms are offered for you to work with, and each of these has a name for reference: *The Rising Light, Walking Participation, Entering Stillness,* and so forth. A summary of the forms described in this book is found in Appendix E.

Learning and practicing the forms is a simple, but exponential process. If you begin with the initial forms described in this chapter, they take only a few minutes to learn, and they develop powerfully with daily practice. Within, say, three weeks, you will have experienced the two primary forms, the *Rising Light* and *Walking Participation*. Everything else follows from these simple beginnings.

The Body of the Tree

In the last thousand years or so, there have been many changes in the way that the Tree of Life is conceived and represented, especially in literature and in the teaching methods from the 19th century to the present day. One of our aims, with these simple but powerful exercises, is to return to primal Qabalah; the other is to work with the Miracle Tree in a way that is utterly contemporary, and so to lay a foundation for future work. In this book we explore Qabalistic forms that are appropriate for the 21st century, bridging between past and future. Such aims are not incompatible, for the Tree of Life is a state of Being, and our participation in that state is based on what we are, rather than what we think, read, or discuss. I say *participation*, for taking part, being consciously aware, is everything in Qabalah. Yet, contrary to popular dogma about meditation and spiritual arts, it is not solely about "higher" consciousness. Through our practices with the Tree, we do indeed come into a deeper and altered awareness, but not by bootstrapping our consciousness, elevating ourselves astrally, or seeking to escape to higher planes and flee from the mundane. The mundane is the most sacred, in all Qabalistic traditions, for it is the manifest shape and presence of the Divine Being that is the source of all things. How can we flee this presence? The answer is that we cannot. To do so would be to deny our very Being. Yet we try to flee it in so many ways, day by day. In this flight we reject and deny ourselves.

One of the most valuable Qabalistic axioms is that the greatest mystery of spiritual truth is present already, in the manifest world. This concept was central to the idea of the Philosophers' Stone, the pivotal quest of the medieval alchemists and Qabalists, which was described as common and omnipresent, yet hidden from all but the most dedicated seekers after Wisdom. As we are such seekers, here and now, the Stone will become apparent to us.

Qabalah is Physical

The Tree of Life works through the human body: all Qabalah is physical. Anyone who denies this has not practiced Qabalah, as the subtle forces always flow through our entire organism. We could say that although we use the words *physical* and *metaphysical* in discussion, both aspects of Being are at one through the body, and are not divided. Only the isolated and disconnected mind makes such divisions, such dualisms, for the body knows them not.

This simple truth is extremely helpful for us, for, if we can grasp it and work with it, it enables us to side-step much of the accumulated junk of magic and metaphysics, and remember our true nature, as participants in the Planet, as Beings who embody the Tree of Life. That is how miracles of transformation begin, though they are, in truth, our normal state of Being. Remember that the way we live is only habitual, and not necessarily our normal or our true potential state.

The Most Powerful Way to Work With the Miracle Tree

Contrary to much that we have all learned, tried, practiced, in our spiritual lives, the most powerful way to work spiritually is while walking around with eyes open. When we do this, we are consciously participating in the holism of our Planet, Moon, and solar system. We do not need to withdraw into a trance or a vision, though visionary work is often used in Qabalah, and can be helpful.

Our contemporary spiritual revival, however, places an unhealthy overemphasis on the vision, the guided meditation, and the withdrawn consciousness. Though we are perhaps unwilling to admit it, this emphasis on inner vision in the last 30 years is closely connected to our visual technology, television, the computer screen, film, video, and so forth. The visual dominates our culture, but it is the artificial visual in so many examples, in the very rhythm of daily life. So the visual has come to dominate much of our spiritual revival (in Western modernist cultures), just as it dominates advertising, entertainment, and media of communication.

In practical work, a simple exercise goes a long way to prove this truth: you can participate fully in the Tree of Life while walking in everyday surroundings with eyes open. This exercise has been done by many of my students in recent years, with excellent, and often surprising, results.

Indeed, this walking exercise or *form* is one of the most powerful, most advanced forms of Qabalistic practice, with a long history of practice rooted in ancient sources. We can never outgrow it, now matter how much our awareness changes through magical or spiritual arts.

So rather than discuss the concept further, here is the exercise for you to try. If you do this once or twice a day, while walking somewhere, it will have a deep transformative effect at all levels of your Being. You do not need to focus on this for long periods of time: "more" is not necessarily better when you work with the Tree of Life. A few minutes each day is enough, and those minutes will deepen, strengthen, and clarify, with regular practice.

Walking Participation

1. *While walking outdoors (anywhere), first prepare yourself by being calm and still as you walk*. This should not be a strenuous effort, but a simple acknowledgement that you are

still, and are ready to change your awareness. This moving into stillness is greatly enhanced by the form called *Entering Stillness*, which is described at the close of this chapter.

2. *Walking normally, look towards the horizon.* If you do not have a horizon, as is often so in the city, look to the distance. Many people walk looking downwards, which can be a difficult habit to dissolve at first. The traditional teaching is "let your eyes rest upon the horizon." We do this so seldom, that when we work with it, it has a powerful effect upon our awareness and our vitality.

3. *As you walk, sense your body through your feet, loins, heart, and head.* This is a simple sensory practice, beginning with the feet, and moving upwards. It is a matter of feeling rather than concentrating. Too much effort will disperse this subtle feeling, which is really about recovering an awareness that we have habitually rejected, rather than building a new form of awareness through willpower or repetition.

4. *As you sense the body, make the following connections: My Feet are in the Earth, my Loins are in the Moon, my Heart is in the Sun, my Head is in the Stars.* This is the point at which we focus on the physical and not the metaphysical. As you participate, think very simply and directly that the physical zones of the body (feet, genitals and hips, heart and chest, shoulders and head) are literally and physically connected to the *physical* Earth, Moon, Sun and Stars. Not symbolically, not through colors or attributes, but literally and physically. This connection is greatly enhanced by

being aware of the general location of Earth, Moon, Sun, and Stars. Does this seem simplistic? Then consider, that while the Earth is always beneath us, and around us to the Four Directions, the Moon, Sun, and Stars move ceaselessly. There is an entire cycle of meditation and Understanding that springs from this concept of movement and relationship, but initially it is the Walking Participation, and nothing else.

5. *Continue with the connection and participation, linking Earth, Moon, Sun, Stars through your body.* If you drift into the symbolic and metaphysical, simply reaffirm the physical connections to physical Earth, Moon, Sun, and Stars. A litany, which you recite silently, can help: "My feet are in the Earth, my loins (genitals) are in the Moon, my heart is in the Sun, and my head is in the Stars."

6. *After some minutes of this, return to being calm and still as you walk, letting your eyes rest upon the horizon.*

If you wish, you can keep a daily journal of what you experience with this form of physical Qabalah. Eventually you will not need the journal, but it is helpful initially to formulate the experiences that you will have.

You will recognize connections between this form and others, such as the *Rising Light*, but do not strive to combine them together in practice. Each form should be practiced simply, directly, uniquely. Only when you have done that, experienced the transformations that it brings, can you begin with combinations of forms. Some, such as *Entering Stillness*, which is a major form (with variants in all spiritual traditions worldwide), can be used before and after any other form, as an opening or closing phase. We will return to this idea of combining forms again. Before then, go for a few walks.

At this stage we have two forms, *Rising Light* and *Walking Participation*. To close this chapter, we will work with the most powerful form of all, the one that we learn at the beginning of our Qabalistic practices, and which remains with us for all of our lives. For this form leads from manifestation into the Void, from Being to Unbeing. It carries us through the entire Tree of Life in one simple exercise, and encompasses all that there is, by stilling all that there is.

Entering Stillness Exercise

This is the classic form, found in various presentations in every spiritual tradition worldwide. If you do nothing else in your life, do this. You will never "outgrow" this form, never advance beyond its potential. This is the first and last form, the shift of consciousness within us that mirrors the universal creation, whereby Being comes out of Unbeing, creation flows out of the Void. With repeated practice it deepens: use this form before any other, in addition to working with it in its own right.

When we try to discuss Entering Stillness, the words are inadequate. But when we participate, employ the form, and enter into stillness, we all recognize that state. It is a form of going home, to the source of our beginning. By stilling time, space, and movement, we come into our full potential.

Sit with eyes closed, free of interruption. With practice you will be able to enter stillness with eyes open, even while moving.

1. Time: withdraw your involvement in time...find yourself time-free, then time-less.
   Space: draw in your awareness from all directions, releasing your involvement with space. Rest on a simple point of Being, within you.
   Movement: Cease all outer and inner movement, except breathing.
2. Reach within yourself to the Unbeing out of which your Being comes. The Stillness that precedes movement, the silence between each breath. This is the Void that is within all things, the source of all Time, Space, and Movement.
3. Let yourself Unbe.
4. Affirm the Four Directions, Above, Below, and Within. (Begin any meditation or ceremony now, or return to your outer awareness).

Assume that all forms begin with Stillness, and practice accordingly. In some forms, described in later chapters, you will find Stillness indicated at key moments in your practice. Once you have discovered how to enter Stillness, through repeated practice, you will find that this form is invaluable, not only as itself, but as a component of your spiritual work overall. The three forms given in this chapter comprise an entire Qabalah of themselves, and you could make them your main practices for some time, before you begin to explore the later forms. The more practiced you are at Stillness, then at the Rising Light and Walking Participation forms, the more effective the other Qabalistic forms and related arts and skills will be for you.

In the next chapter, we will begin our exploration of the Emanations of the Tree of Life, and discover some forms for working with angels.

Chapter 2

Emanations

The Qabalistic Worldview: Models of the World and Information Technology

Working with the Tree of Life, within any Qabalistic tradition, introduces us to models of the world. By this phrase "models of the world" we should mean working models of the universe, patterns of potential that give us ways of relating. This is all that any conceptual model offers, be it scientific, religious, mystical, or day by day practical. The Miracle Tree offers more, however, for it reveals ways of transformation: by changing the way we relate to the world, we change ourselves. The human being is a subtly responsive, ever-changing pattern of interactions, and so is the Tree of Life. Neither we, nor the Tree, are rigid. But the human being likes to have patterns, to have a model or structure that gives us ways of relating, not just of describing or explaining. Information and explanations alone are not sufficient for us, we must also relate, and having related, we must participate. If we do not relate and participate, even the most voluminous flood of information cannot give us back our lives. In an "information culture" we often forget that data, information, is not life, and thus we attempt to reduce aspects of life to mere data. Yet when we do so, this digital substitute for living is arid, fruitless, and deeply frustrating. So we cry for more data, just as children cry for more sugar.

The exaggerated value placed on information, and rapid access to information, is a major feature of our computer-driven society. Closely linked with the idea that more information is good, is the barely concealed implication of control. If only we had the maximum information, the reasoning goes, we could control our situation more effectively. Yet, as we acquire more information, we discover that we cannot control the world in the simplistic infantile manner that is implied. The most revealing examples of this are in the life cycles of the planetary environment, and, mirrored small, in the cycles of human disease. In the first, that of the environment, we have discovered that the planetary entity is extremely sensitive to human input, and, in the short term, is easily damaged. More recently we have discovered that vast planetary forces of adjustment come into play when we create imbalances, and that these work over long periods of time. Where is the human control in such a scenario? How will our information benefit us, other than to reveal that which we cannot control? What we must find are ways of cooperation and participation.

The notion that human science can dominate and control nature was supreme for two centuries or more: now it is shown to be absurd and self-destructive. Yet it is perpetuated incessantly, with a terrible fervor. We *are* the environment; if we disrupt it, damage it, poison it, we attack ourselves. The human immune system mirrors this truth: through our obsession with control and dominance in medicine, we have pushed the immune system to the brink. Combative medicine has caused both humans and microorganisms to change rapidly in response to drugs and antibiotics. The presumed advances and medical certainties of one or two generations past no longer apply, and we live in a world where "eliminated" diseases return and complex syndromes proliferate. So much for information and control, and the delusion that all illness shall be banished by science.

Information is only helpful if we use it with Understanding and Wisdom: on the Tree of Life the supernal spheres of Understanding and Wisdom encompass and emanate all others. Yet we constantly apply knowledge and its lesser component of data or information, simply because we have it, regardless of Understanding, Wisdom, or deeper insights, which are rejected intentionally for short-term ends. If information is employed solely for purposes of instant gratification or of manipulative control, the benefits are very short term indeed. Furthermore, this concept of the value of information has changed substantially in the computer era. Not long ago, information or data was an auxiliary of knowledge, was understood to be a means towards certain ends, be they known or unknown. This has changed, for the pursuit and acquisition of data becomes an end in itself, replacing our human insight and Wisdom with a simplistic logic machine. Computers are good servants, but bad masters.

As we hurtle through this accelerated phase of the Information Age, a few people gain short-term benefits. But the very nature of information technology, and the implied control, means that the majority does not benefit: we become data-fodder, units, consumers, and statistics. Never people, never participators. Our role is increasingly passive.

Occultism Previewed Computer Culture

Curiously, but not surprisingly, this obsession with gathering and sorting data was prevalent in 19th and 20th century occultism. It is still dominant today in the majority of methods, books, and classes, based on the Tree of Life and Qabalah. To many people, Qabalah in any tradition, but especially the Western or Hermetic, offers a mass of highly intellectualized systematized information...yet the bulk of it is frustrating and incomprehensible. It is because information has been valued over participation. Accumulate comparisons, hold them at arms length, study them, and find the "complete system." This obsession of occultism previewed exactly what we find today in our computer driven culture.

If you were given an entire library of all the Qabalistic texts ever written, published and unpublished, what would you do? Spend years reading it? Exhaust your energies hunting for the one, the one and only, book (hidden somewhere in the stacks or on disc) that had the *true* information? A tenth of the time and energy spent in meditation with the Tree of Life would transform us utterly. The true text is within us, just as we are truly within the universal Being.

The Latest Breakthrough is Best...

In our modernist society, we often assume that the latest breakthrough in science is literally the most up to date truth. Yet it is nothing more than an amended model, based upon a stance, a position, and a starting place...a theoretical worldview. We easily overlook the historical perspective, forgetting that each and every scientific model of the past has been replaced; yet each was adequate and fulfilling for the people that shared its conceptual model.

Furthermore, wc live, day by day, using the benefits obtained for us by these earlier, now disproven and outmoded scientific models and worldviews; we hardly ever think of the paradox inherent in this scenario.

The idea of *relationship* holds good for all world-views or models. It is not so much a matter of their accuracy, for such accuracy is relative and ephemeral, but of their value to us as models of relationship to, and of participation within, the greater world of which our human world is a small part. In the immediate sense, this greater world is Planet Earth, the 10th sphere, the Kingdom. But it is also the Solar World, the Stellar World, and the universe within which our Star, our Sun, our Earth, lives and participates.

From the False to the True

There is an old meditational exercise, once taught to initiates, in which the individual works to create an absurd worldview, based on a simple starting thesis. Indeed, this is the basis of one the earliest Christian propagandas...we believe because it is absurd. Once you have seeded an absurd worldview, you develop and extend it in meditation, and it will begin to open out your comprehension of the world. You will have realizations, insights, understandings that relate strongly to the outer world, and which have surprisingly practical applications, all stemming from an absurd starting point. Beginning with that which is "false," we find that it leads us towards that which is "true." This curious law of consciousness holds good in another, more sinister manner. Begin with some absurd propaganda, slowly control and change the information available to people, steer and limit their choices so that they are not aware of any alternative understanding of how to live, and you have created a new world, and captured a large number of people to live in it, under your rules. Of course, no one does this.

To pursue the idea of models and worldviews further: our contemporary model of physics, for example, is based on advanced mathematical theory. It does not offer ways of participating in the universe, so much as ways of describing a theoretical universe that may or may not relate to the manifest world of Suns, Moons and Planets, and Stars. Some years ago I attend a fascinating talk by a leading American physicist, who was employed by a major corporation to explore what may or may not occur in sub-nuclear realms. He cheerfully told us that millions of dollars were being spent on something "entirely theoretical with no practical relationship to anything whatsoever." The value of such abstract knowledge may seem less than relevant, and the cost of obtaining it may seem profligate, in a world that is dying through human abuse, yet we pursue this knowledge assiduously while millions starve and die. But of course, it may have military applications in the future, if we can acquire enough data on it.

Despite our modernist obsession with new developments in science, we still use the older models of both a mechanistic and an electrical reality (each quite different from one another, yet both describing the same world) in our day-to-day applications for the countless processes of modern society—our machines, our communications, our travel, our household appliances. We do not stop to think that the science that created these devices is already out of date, and based on worldviews that have been superseded. Such "old" scientific models still work, and the development of further, perhaps more sophisticated models, does not stop them from working. That which is, apparently, proven to be untrue or inadequate as a theoretical description of the world, does not cease to work within practical parameters. Science, especially, has shown this to be so, over and over again.

All Models of the World Work

This brings us to a deeply significant concept: *all models of the world work*. We are free to choose whichever model we wish. By making such choices, our interaction with the world will vary, and our conscious participation in the life of the world will change. Thus we might expand the concept: *all models of the world work, and we change according to our participation within any such model.* Models of the world have a specific tone or "flavor"...if you attune to a model, you will acquire its flavor, and you will change accordingly.

Of the many models that humanity has created through the ages, the Tree of Life, the Qabalistic worldview, is the most open-ended and inclusive. It has the curious property that any other model, any worldview, can be located somewhere upon the Tree, and given a context within the Qabalistic model. This conceptual property is unique, and none of the religious or materialistic models, including those of psychology, act in this manner. Yet, to the practicing Qabalist, it is not so surprising. The Tree of Life is a description of *that which is present,* offering a model of relationships between different aspects of that which is present. As such, all other models will fit within its parameters. To allow this wondrous aspect of the Tree of Life to come alive, we must participate in a Qabalistic world-view. Not acquire information on it, but live within it. As it is an open-ended and changeable worldview (rather than a rigid complete system, as we are often misinformed), it liberates us from our delusions of control, and brings us into a greater world, of which our human world is a reflection in miniature.

Emanations, Planets, Worlds

In this section we will explore the concept of the spheres or *sephiroth* of the Tree of Life. Literature has rendered this simple concept complex, and as always, the burden of 19th century occultism has been one of confusion and of excessive attention to comparative detail. While texts that list the attributes of the Tree repeat one another, and generally offer similar information, the welter of detail gives little in the way of insight or practical experience. If we begin, continue, and conclude with the key concept that we are already the Tree of Life, we can approach the Tree afresh, and rediscover ways of working that have been forgotten, and explore new ways, apt for our time.

It is, of course, possible to work with the Tree of Life merely as a mental exercise: at this level it is similar to those simulated worlds generated by computer software, in which basic mathematics and pattern-making abilities can be applied to vastly complex reiterations which are essentially arid or abstract. Qabalah works at many interwoven levels of living consciousness, and the mental iterations and patterns, which are the main subjects of occult literature, are merely one-tenth of one-tenth of the Tree of Life (the Mercurial mental forms of the 8th sphere, the sphere of Scintillation or Brilliance). If this seems strange, it will become clear as this chapter progresses!

The Spheres or Emanations

There are 10 spheres, or *sephiroth*, or Emanations on a typical Tree of Life. The traditional term *Emanation* is helpful for us, as the word "sphere" is often used loosely in western books on Qabalah without going into the implications and potentials of the concept of Emanation. In this book, both *sphere* and *Emanation* are used interchangeably, in a manner similar to the Hebrew word *sephiroth*. Sephiroth is often translated as Emanations, and the sephiroth could also be termed cosmic aspects of the divine universal Being.

Before we explore each sphere or Emanation, we should consider, afresh, what they are, and wherefrom they emanate. Firstly, the Emanations are not merely colored circles of symbolism in a numbered sequence. They are alive, they are interconnected, and they mutually enfold one another. The sequential nature of flat illustrations on a printed page gives an illusion of separation. Regrettably, the printed illustration is often used as a starting point for Qabalistic exploration, which was never its intended use. The Tree of Life is really unlike the customary illustrations *(Figure 1)*, but they are so deeply entrenched in the published texts, that we are obliged to work with them. In this book you will find some alternative models for the Tree of Life, and a number of forms or methods of spiritual transformation that use these other, equally valid and effective, models. Nowadays we have the graphic potential in computers to radically improve the visual presentation of the Tree of Life, especially in three dimensions with rotation and color. However, to do this successfully, the designer has to be a practicing Qabalist, and must reach beyond the customary illustrations that are found in general publication.

The Tenfold Pattern

Traditionally, Qabalists have laid emphasis upon the tenfold pattern. When something is enshrined in tradition, it is our task to respect its potential Wisdom, but also to explore it thoroughly, and not merely accept it dogmatically. Wisdom traditions share certain truths worldwide, for such truths are properties or aspects of consciousness seeking to explore and relate to the manifest and unmanifest worlds. When we find certain themes repeated through the centuries, and across different cultures, we may pursue the kernel of insight within them. The long tradition of a decimal Tree of Life is one such theme.

The Tree of Life is not a picture of circles and lines, but a subtly simple decimal cosmology. This is not surprising, for it comes to us from ancient sources such as those received by Pythagoras and Plato, and from Sufi (Arabic) tradition, all of which used decimal mathematics. The modern decimal system comes directly out of these Wisdom traditions. They themselves are founded upon an ancient perennial Wisdom tradition, based on observation of universal (stellar) patterns combined with deep contemplation of the nature of consciousness and Being.

Decimal metaphysics was incorporated into Jewish mysticism in the Middle Ages, during the Golden Age in Spain, when Arab, Jewish, and Christian mystics and scientists freely exchanged knowledge with one another. At this time, it was the Arab world that had preserved much of the Wisdom of ancient Greece, and that reintroduced it to the west. Within this decimal cosmology, described as the ten spheres or Emanations, there is a simpler and older triple pattern: that of Three Triads, three sets of three Emanations, the whole Tree of Life being a triple unit, with the Triads as its components. This Unit, *in its totality*, makes the Tenth. The concept of Emanations is deeply rooted in the Triads, which reflect one another through all creation into manifestation. Traditionally, this is described as 3x3=9, plus the totality of 9 as a unity or whole (1), making both 1 and 10. From this 10 or this 1, we begin again, in a further cycle of 10, ad infinitum.

Thus the utterance or issuing of the Tree of Life out of the Void, of Being out of Unbeing, is understood by the Qabalist as a sequence of three interacting Triads of relationship...not a linear progression of ten separate entities. The linear progression is a matter of human philosophers counting in sequence, not of Emanations in the process towards manifestation. We could liken the difference to traveling on a train: when you are making the journey you think of it station by station, and this is how it presents itself to you, in a linear sequence. Yet the entire network and all the stations are present, and form a totality that we cannot comprehend if we limit ourselves to the step-by-step checklist. If we alter our perspective, however, we can discover the totality, be it of a rail network or of the Tree of Life.

When you work with a Tree of Life, think always of Three Triads, within one another, flowing from one to the other, never separate, never linear. If you have this in your meditations, you are a true Qabalists, and none of the miracles of the Tree will be far from you.

The Three Triads

The first Triad is that of Being, Wisdom, and Understanding, often called the Supernal or Stellar spheres. Being is androgynous, while Wisdom and Understanding have an interchange of polarity between them. At this deep level of the origins of Being, Wisdom and Understanding are polarized, but are still mutually interchangeable. They do not have a fixed polarity, but are interacting constantly, and through their interactions creating polarity that is defined as the second Triad.

Being is the universal divine entity that comprises All. Understanding is the vessel of Time and Space that Being emanates, while Wisdom is the power of the Stars that move through Time and Space. This supernal Triad is often cast as the One Divinity (androgynous), the Great Mother (Understanding) and the Star Father (Wisdom).

In this mythic mode, we can relate many traditions of gods and goddesses to the supernal Triad. None are correct, and all are equally valid.

The second Triad is that of Beauty, Severity, and Mercy. These are the Solar spheres. Think of them, and meditate upon them, as being interwoven, not as separate entities. Beauty or Harmony, the 6th sphere, is a direct reflection and Emanation of the 1st sphere, that of Being. Severity is an Emanation of Understanding, and Mercy is an Emanation of Wisdom. The Solar Triad is, in its totality, an Emanation of the Stellar Triad. Meditate upon this mutual reflection between the Stellar and Solar Triads *(See figure 4, pg. 36)*.

The third Triad is that of Foundation, Brilliance, and Exaltation. These are the Lunar spheres. The Foundation or 9th sphere (but really the interaction of 9th and 10th spheres, a theme which we will explore later in this chapter) is a direct reflection and Emanation of Beauty, the 6th sphere. The Lunar Triad is, in its totality, an Emanation of the Solar Triad. Meditate upon this mutual reflection between the Solar and Lunar Triads.

The 10th sphere or Kingdom, is the sum of the three Triads, and not a separate sphere or entity in itself. It is shown on the standard flat-plan Tree of Life as a separate sphere, representing Planet Earth. For us the Kingdom is Planet Earth (and our bodies) because that is where we are! The Kingdom is, of course, all manifest worlds throughout the universe: the sum of the Stellar, Solar, Lunar Triads of all Stars in time and space.

As the Tree of Life comes to us from both philosophical and metaphysical visionary traditions, we soon discover that number plays an important role in its Wisdom. But not a dogmatic or an occult role: number ramifications became an obsession for both oriental and western

Qabalists, often excluding other spiritual practices. The secret of number is thus: it underpins creation. All science, all physics, is based on this truth. Yet we do not need to "know" the secrets of either higher mathematics or of esoteric numerology to work with the Tree of Life. Why? Because we are, already, those numbers, those forces, those relationships. Number underpins creation; it works for us, with us, and within us, continually. If you are seeking to "crack the code," you are not practicing Qabalah, for you are still working from an external place. Discover that you are the code; let it live within you...what is there to crack?

Living the Tree: Participation

This book is full of forms. But these are of no use whatsoever unless they occur within our life...not as special activities on weekends, or on occasions, but within our life day by day, moment by moment. The idea of inclusion, of participation, is central to Qabalah. The Miracle Tree cannot work fully for us if we exclude ourselves from it by distractions, and, most of all, by lack of participation. If we are not consciously participating, then our interactions with the Tree return to an unconscious level, the level of the ancestral and biological life processes. If we consciously participate, these forces awaken within us, especially in our bodies, and provide infinite resources of energy. This "secret" is found in many traditions worldwide, and forms the Foundation for all practical Qabalah. *There are direct ways for the Living Spirit to work through the body: all we need to do is willingly take part.*

Let us consider how this process unfolds on the Tree itself. We will work with each of the three Triads, looking for simple meditational material that might support us in daily life. These are merely initial clues and proposal; with practice, you will unerringly find your own living meditations on the ten spheres, the Triads of Emanations.

The Lunar Triad and Earth

10th Emanation: The Earth

The world of nature is already paradise. If we remember that we are included in this world, and not in conflict with it, our bodies will adjust to the rhythms of Earth and Moon, tides and weather. This does not imply "going back to nature," but a process of being aware that we are in nature now. Many of the forms in this book work directly through the body, and will greatly enhance our awareness of the natural world. Because all parts of the Tree of Life are connected to one another, a so-called "advanced" or "higher" spiritual practice can never be divorced from the body. That is the very reason why we are born into this world, to realize the Kingdom of Heaven on Earth, the utter presence of the Crown in the Kingdom, of Divine Spirit in Radiant Substance. In practice, all the forms flow into the 10th sphere, the Kingdom/Queendom, and will have transformative effects that work through the body.

9th Emanation: The Moon, Power of Foundation

We will not be able to relate to the Moon while we think of it as a dead lump orbiting Earth, as a chunk of sterile real estate. The physical Moon is the scribing point that hews out the true 9th sphere, which is the totality of the Moon's movements around Earth. The Moon inscribes a sphere around us perpetually, with its orbits: we live, literally, within the Moon. The Earth is in the Moon. In older forms of Qabalah and related cosmology, the Foundation was understood to be Earth and Moon combined, while the Kingdom was the material form of the entire universe. This is often overlooked in contemporary Qabalah, and the Moon is thought of as being "one step up" from Earth. Do not conceive of the Lunar realm as being somehow separate from the world of nature: we live within it always. Its tides, rhythms, and forces are all about us, day and night, and within us. Tides of the ocean, of water, of blood. Tides of emotion, of sexuality, of dreams, and longing. We live within these, and they are far more than some shadowy segment of our psyche. Indeed, the frantic pace of human modernist culture is a collective acceleration, as is the population growth. These derive from lunar forces, drawing up a flood tide of humanity.

To live with the Moon, we have to be aware of tides. Of ebbing and flowing, of giving and receiving. These tides are in the individual body, mind, and emotions, just as much as they are in the deep oceans and the breeding cycles of all living creatures.

8th Emanation: Mercury, power of Brilliance, Thought, Mind

In the 8th sphere we come into Brilliance, and our minds become swift. In an abstract sense this is the realm of thought (thought without emotion). There are many ways for us to enhance our mental processes, most of them work through interaction with one of the other spheres of the Miracle Tree…and clarity of mind comes as a result of this interaction. It is less effective to work "direct" upon mind, thought, Brilliance, though in Qabalistic meditation there are ways to do so. One of the many "secrets" of working with the Tree is that you develop and grow in one sphere through interaction with those around it, not working directly on that sphere itself. The Tree of Life is often said to be a universal map showing the spheres and connecting Paths of the universe, the solar system, and the human body. Indeed this type of approach is classic 8th sphere Brilliance: mapping a network and using the flow of forces in the entire network to adjust one point upon it.

In daily living we find ourselves in a culture that functions primarily through the end results of the 8th sphere: Science. In a modernist society, technology is all. With only a few moments of Thought, we can conclude that the emphasis upon technology and machinery in pursuit of profit is imbalanced. Not necessarily wrong or evil, but out of control. Of course, technology is only one aspect of this sphere, but it is the dominant at this time in human history. Meditations on the 8th sphere should include regular explorations of Appropriateness. How appropriate is our use of technology, both collective and individual? How much do we define ourselves as individuals by our machines?

7th Emanation: Venus, power of Exaltation, Triumph, Achievement

Venus is the realm of the emotions, especially associated with *feeling*, through its sensuous exchange of energies. The 7th sphere meditations are often those of both detachment and commitment. Meditational detachment in the sense of observing our feelings, our sensuous inclinations, rather than being driven by them. Living commitment in the sense that we must experience the spirit of Exaltation before we have any true Understanding of its power. This polarized pattern is typical of Venus, attraction towards, and movement away from, any focus of attention. The "secret" of daily work with this sphere is that we do not own our Exaltation. This is the true Triumph of Venus…we discover that the potent forces are non-personal, and that they flow according to certain laws. Once we cross this threshold, we are no longer bound by delusions of Achievement, but have achieved liberation.

The Solar Triad

6th Emanation: Sun, power of Beauty, Harmony, and Balance

Just as the glamour of Venus is ruthlessly popularized and commercialized, so is the idea of beauty. The Beauty of the 6th sphere is that of harmony, of being at the center of interactions, rather than whirled around on the Wheel of Fortune. Regular meditations on this sphere could begin with considering the difference between glamour and beauty in our culture. But the core meditation is that of Stillness, coming into the central Light of peace.

5th Emanation: Mars, power of Severity, Discipline, Purification

The 5th sphere is that of Severity, of necessary cleansing and elimination. In modernist society, we oscillate between the binges of greed and indulgence, and the egocentric obsessions with dieting and purification. Meditations on Severity in our culture could begin with discovering the difference between discipline and violence, between Severity and cruelty, between self-obsession and purity. From there we could move into the deeper nature of Severity: that which limits and cleanses, the catabolic power within all things. How do we find this healthy balancing force within us? By attuning to the inner spirit of Mars, which works through the cleansing forces of the blood.

4th Emanation: power of Jupiter, Mercy, Generosity, and Expansion

The 4th sphere gives, grows, and grants all. It is the building, anabolic power in the cosmos. So, of course, we want it all, and we want it now. Yet some of our worst diseases are examples of the power of the 4th sphere running unabated, without the limits of the 5th. Cancer is a disease of the 4th sphere, manifesting through the 9th or Foundation, into a proliferation and growth of cells. Interestingly, it is arrested or cured through purity and transformation of the blood, the agent of the 5th sphere or Mars. Meditations on the 4th sphere could begin with exploring the delusion of endless growth and expansion that corrodes the heart of our culture. Only dramatic martial forces, such as war, stop this delusion. Can we not find a way to Mercy in this endless seesaw of greed and violence?

At a deeper level, we move into the spiritual consciousness of compassion. At this level many reputedly "good" things are seen in a new light, more as cancerous accretions than as true benefits.

The Stellar Triad

3rd Emanation: Saturn, power of Understanding, the Great Mother, Ocean of Time and Space

In the human world, Understanding is often an agonizing process. We simply do not understand much that goes on around us and within us. We long for Understanding from others, but often cannot give it ourselves. As we age, we find that a measure of Understanding comes with experience. This slow and painful Path to Understanding takes many lifetimes, often of pain and suffering. This is, like it or not, our general individual and collective situation. Or is it?

We all know that other Understanding, where we suddenly comprehend something without explanation, data, or hardship. Often this deeper Understanding is linked to intuition. The quality of intuition is often of Understanding

(3rd Emanation) flowing into the dream pool, the collective Foundation of consciousness (9th Emanation). Both Understanding and Wisdom have a primal presence, as a combined androgynous consciousness, in the sphere of the Moon.

In Qabalistic tradition, we discover how to commune directly with the universal Understanding. This is different from experiential Understanding, and from intuitive Understanding. It is the source of both. We might begin our daily meditations with ideas of Understanding, long term cycles of planetary consciousness, of our place in the vast universe of time, space and Stars: such meditations are correctives to our usual frantic humanocentric concerns. But we should move on to direct absorption within the universal Understanding. This is done through Stillness, and through wordless, formless "feeling" our way into the unqualified consciousness that simply comprehends, only understands. Without subject, without object.

2nd Emanation: Neptune, power of Wisdom, the patterns of Stars and Planets moving Within the Universe

As with Understanding, we usually come to Wisdom through experience. Sometimes a young child will exhibit the classic Wisdom of Innocence. The Wisdom of Innocence arises because the child is close the source of Being (1st Emanation), wherefrom Wisdom flows.

We might begin our Wisdom meditations by contemplating cycles, patterns, and universal Laws of Being. If we were to apply such contemplation to the way we interact with our Planet, we would indeed by coming into Wisdom. But we do not, and our folly is not that of Innocence. From this initial set of meditations, we can move into the concept of wordless, formless, Wisdom. This is a universal flow of consciousness, within which all things swim...nebulae, stars, worlds, living beings, we. Open yourself to Wisdom, and it will flow through you. Harden yourself to it, and in Time, it will crack you open. The choice is ours, always.

1st Emanation: Uranus, power of Crown, Being, First Beginning of All

Traditionally it is associated with the swirling nebulae issuing out of the Void, just as Wisdom is associated with the Zodiac, as a set of patterns of universal power.

Here we have the Stillness form, and simply Being. Nothing more, Nothing less.

A Summary of the Emanations

Let us move on now to some further explorations of the Emanations:

10th Emanation or sphere: The Earth

As far as we are concerned, it is our Planet Earth. It is our manifesting place, our starting and finishing place. As a Planet, it embodies the Universal Spiritual forces of The Kingdom...these forces are present in all manifestation. Thus any star, planet, rock, or speck of dust, is the Kingdom; the entire manifest universe is the Kingdom. But for us, in our Solar System, we experience the forces of the 10th sphere on and through Planet Earth. Earth is our manifest world. But when you meditate upon a Tree of Life, also remember that the Kingdom is the totality of the three Triads, the unit of those three threes. It is the combination of One, the original Being or Crown, and Zero, the Unmanifest out of which the One creates the manifest universe.

On a meditational Tree of Life, such as a picture or wall hanging, the 10th Emanation shows the Wheel of Change, or the Four Elements and Four Seasons, with a rainbow or fourfold color pattern (*see Appendix C*). The four quarters represent the Life phases, the cycle of the Sun, and the four archangels that are "closest" to Earth. But they also show the interaction of time, space, and movement, which shapes the entire universe.

The fourfold spiritual powers of Life, Light, Love, and Law, become the four elements of Air, Fire, Water, and Earth. In contemporary terms, the Kingdom shows a set of interactions and iterations. Such is the nature of our world.

9th Emanation or sphere: the Moon, Foundation

Not the physical satellite (for that is part of the Kingdom) but the subtle forces of creation and destruction that are woven around our Planet Earth, and embodied or mediated by the movement of our physical satellite, the Moon. This lunar sphere of energies, within which we live and move and have our Being, is the true Foundation. It is the interaction of Earth and Moon, of 10th and 9th Emanations. The lunar forces are those that bring entities into manifestation, and take them out of manifestation. They are the tides of creation and destruction at the very threshold of matter, of manifestation into and out of form.

Thus the 9th sphere has its counterpart or organ in our solar system, as our Moon, but has a universal presence as the Foundation upon which all manifestation rests, and through which all form returns on its way back to original energy or force. The 9th Emanation is associated with the color of deep violet, and with the lunar metal and color of silver.

We should meditate first upon the lunar sphere in context of Earth: it is the Foundation of our Kingdom. The physical Moon, weaving its ceaseless orb about our Planet, is our immediate source of Foundational spiritual energies. In the older traditions of Qabalah, the combined entity of Planet Earth and Moon comprised the Foundation, while all manifestation, universally, was the Kingdom. This reminds us of the triple pattern inherent within the Tree, the three Triads, mirroring one another (*see figure 1, pg. 33*). To grasp this, let us return briefly to the concept of the Triads. A Tree of Life could be understood as consisting solely of Foundation, Center, and Crown. These are the Triads, with Foundation as spheres 10–9/8/7, Center or Harmony, as spheres 6/5/4, and Crown or Being, as spheres 3/2/1.

The third Triad on the Tree is that of Brilliance (Mercury), Exaltation (Venus) and Foundation (Moon). These are the forces of thinking, feeling, and manifestation into form. This entire Triad appears physically as our Planet Earth, and as the body/mind/emotion complex of any living creature. The Foundation is the totality of this Triad.

8th Emanation or sphere: Mercury, Brilliance or Scintillation

Not the physical Planet, for that is part of the Kingdom, but the energies that are mediated by the Planet Mercury into and out of our solar system. The planetary attributes of the Tree of Life are not, as is often stated, "symbols." They indicate which universal forces are mediated in and out of the Solar system by which Planets. Think of the Planets and their attendant satellites as mediating points, or organs of the Solar Being. As soon as you have this in your meditations, all confusion over lists of "symbols" can be disposed of. The Planets do not represent or symbolize anything; they do things. The physical Planets are the Kingdom—aspects of the inner powers of the Emanations. In another solar system, the same forces would be mediated by different entities, according to the pattern emitted by that Star. They would be the same Emanations, however, as these are universal.

Mercury embodies scintillating movement of mind, of analytical interacting consciousness without emotion. It mediates that universal realm of thought that connects swiftly. In our solar system it is the fast moving Planet, in our consciousness it is clarity and activity of thought. The 8th sphere is the realm of "connection through thought" while its polar partner, Venus, the 7th sphere is the realm of "connection through feeling."

Traditionally the 8th Emanation has a brilliant orange color, and is further associated with the metal and the scintillating color of Mercury.

7th Emanation or sphere: Venus, Exaltation, Ecstasy, and Victory

We might also meditate on ecstasy, triumph, and the much-used idea of Victory, all of which are feelings or energetic modes that arise from communion with this sphere.

The Planet Venus mediates the forces of connection through feeling that flow into and out of our solar system, our Planet, and our bodies. It is the node or organ of the universal sphere of Exaltation. Venus has a direct connection to the body, to the Planet, through *touch*: this is why the archangel of the 7th Emanation, Auriel, is also archangel of the element of Earth in our bodily and planetary manifestation. We will explore this further in our section on angels and archangels.

This sphere of Exaltation manifests for us as our feelings, with a strong connection to the sensuous, to touch.

When the forces of the 7th sphere flow outwards to manifest, they move into the element of Earth, touching and
feeling. When they flow inwards, towards the spiritual
spheres of Being, they move away from Earth towards
Fire, and the sensuous aspects are repatterned as ecstasy
or exaltation. This is why sex is associated with Venus, for
it brings both physically sensuous peaks of energy, and
spiritual ecstasy. Many of the forms and practices associated with Qabalah focus on the idea of *direction*. Does the
energy move outwards or inwards? Can we consciously
move it? Are we aware of its movement?

The 7th Emanation is shown by radiant green, and also
by the metal and the color of copper.

6th Emanation or sphere: The Sun, Beauty, Harmony, and Balance

Now we are meditating upon a different class of entity, for the Sun is a Star. The Sun is the focus of the solar
Triad (Sun, Mars, Jupiter, Beauty, Severity, Mercy). It is
also the center of the solar system, the greater Being within
which we have our Earth Life. In traditional Qabalah and
magical arts, the term Solar Logos is often found, for the
Sun is the great entity that creates the lesser entities of the
Planets and Moons, and the life forms thereon. This Solar
Logos is an Emanation or Aspect of the Divine Being, the
universal Logos. Thus the Sun is often called the Child of
Light, or the divine Son of God. It is from this esoteric
tradition that the exoteric symbolism and myths of many
religions have come. But remember that it describes a
simple fact: the Stars are born out of the unmanifest, and
they in turn create solar systems. Astronomy and modern
physics, both children of the older magical arts, make the
same statements, albeit in different vocabulary. And how
could they not? Both worldviews describe the same universe, the same processes and patterns.

Our Sun mediates the power of Harmony and Balance from the universal realm of Being, into the specific realm of the solar system. The traditional name for the 6th Emanation is Beauty. This is not glamour or prettiness, but the beauty of balance, harmony, and proportion. The 6th Emanation is also that of the heart, not in romance or personal emotion, but as an organ of life-giving forces at the center of all things. In our solar system, this is the central Star, our Sun. Its physical presence is the outer body for its spiritual presence.

The Beauty of the 6th Emanation is both the balance and the source of the 5th, which is Severity/Destruction and the 4th, which is Mercy/Creation. This is the solar Triad of the Tree of Life.

Much of our work with the forms and practices of Qabalah consists of moving our individual energies from their customary focus within the lunar Triad, into the solar Triad. Not leaving the lunar Triad behind, but merging its forces into the solar Triad. This should not be so difficult, as the lunar Triad is already within the solar, just as Moon and Earth are already in the solar system, just as we are already living on Earth, within the spheres of Moon and Sun. The classic meditational tool of three concentric spheres, shown graphically as three circles, demonstrates this concept *(see figure 2, pg. 34).*

The 6th Emanation, the Sun, Beauty, radiates the solar color of shining gold.

5th Emanation or sphere: Mars, Severity, Discipline

Mars (part of the infinite manifest Kingdom) is the node or mediating organ of universal forces of Severity. Our universe is a set of interactions, of polarized forces. This truth, well known to Qabalists for millennia, has recently been "discovered" by modern science, and has always been clearly shown upon the Tree of Life. The 5th sphere is the Emanation of Severity, of destruction, that which breaks down patterns. It is balanced (6th power) by the 4th Emanation of Mercy, that which builds up patterns.

The forces of the Solar Triad are pure forces: they have no "personality." They work on a level that is not aware of us as humans, for we are minute reflections of these cosmic forces. When they are mirrored into the Lunar Triad, they will convolute into personalities, our masks of habit, self, and ignorance. We can see this in the popular misconceptions of the solar Emanations, and in our misuse of the forces. Mars, Severity, in this miscon-ceived role is "the god of war." We must use force to achieve our ends. The idea of force and control runs through every aspect of modernist culture, and is not lim-ited to the more obvious military conflicts.

This phrase, "god of war" says it all, summarizing many of the ills of our human culture. In the esoteric tradition, the 5th sphere is that of a *goddess* of purification and destruc-tion. In popular mythology, in history, and in the common consciousness, Mars has become a *god* of war.

The pure force of the 5th sphere becomes convoluted through a sense of personal self, and generates the idea of *conflict for selfish ends*, rather than *purification for selfless ends*. This convolution also occurs in the 7th Emanation, where Exaltation becomes associated with Victory (over a defeated enemy) and in the 8th, where swiftness or Bril-liance becomes associated with Glory (of the inflated ego).

It is only through Severity, the cleansing power of the 5th sphere, that we lose these unhealthy imbalanced con-volutions: usually this cleansing comes with death, when the personality is dissolved. As we might expect, the 5th Emanation, Severity, has the color of red blood.

4th Emanation or sphere: Jupiter, Mercy, Giving

The Planet Jupiter is part of the Kingdom of our Solar Being, our Sun. It embodies, and acts as a mediator for, those cosmic forces of expansion, construction, and growth, that run through the entire universe. Upon the Tree of Life, this is the Emanation of Mercy, of giving. In development of the human soul, this is the realm of compassion, the highest spiritual quality that we may express. Traditionally, this sphere is the realm of certain saints or spiritual mentors of humanity who remain within its consciousness out of compassion for us. This is an important feature of traditional Qabalah, and the practical Qabalist will often seek inner contact with these exalted spiritual beings.

The Emanation of Mercy is one of giving. It is that natural force of expansion and proliferation that creates universally, just as its polar partner, Severity, is a natural force of contraction, reduction, and cleansing. It is the balance of these forces, the 4th and 5th spheres, that holds our solar system in place, and gives us our cycle of life, death, and rebirth. Too close to the Sun and we burn, too far from the Sun and we freeze. The forces of expansion and contraction, however, also hold the Stars in flight, not merely the cycle of human lives on Earth.

The 4th Emanation is the first to cross the Abyss of Time, Space, and Motion that separates our Star from any other. For us, it is the last Emanation before we cross the Abyss of death and forgetting. Its Mercy is not only creative, but also forgiving. The 4th Emanation, Mercy, shines with a radiant sky blue.

3rd Emanation or sphere: Saturn, Understanding, the Great Mother

While the Planet Saturn is of the Kingdom or manifest world of our solar system, it embodies and mediates universal Understanding. This Emanation of Understanding is also the infinite ocean of Space and Time, through which the Stars move. The expansion and movement of the Stars is the presence of the 2nd Emanation, that of Wisdom. Traditionally the 3rd sphere is associated with the Dark Mother, the Great goddess who draws all unto herself. This contracting or summoning power shapes and patterns the expanding forces of the universe. Qabalah long predated modern physics with a deep Understanding that the universe is the result of the interactions of time, space, and movement (energy).

When working with this Emanation, we must dispose of the neo-masculine stereotypical overlays associated with Saturn, as a jealous father god who devours his children. It has no place on the Tree of Life, though it is, of course, the corrupt inversion of the Understanding of the Great Mother. We might be tempted to see an intentional manipulation of a powerful mythic theme in the transformations of both the 3rd and 5th Emanations from goddesses to gods, from balance to imbalance. Yet, from a deeper perspective, it is more likely to reflect changes in human culture, politics, and history, changes that eventually lead us away from Understanding, and into our obsession with mere data that dominates us today. In this context we should remember that Time is the property of the 3rd Emanation: one of the hallmarks of modernist culture is that there is never "enough time," along with the associated demands that everything be instantaneous.

The 3rd Emanation brings us into contemplation of the stellar cycles of time, and draws us out of the human concerns of the Lunar Triad into the realm of universal consciousness. Yet, typical to many of the "secrets" of the Tree of Life, the Wisdom and Understanding of the supernal spheres are present in the 9th Emanation, the Foundation, the Moon. Here they appear as the deep cycles of organic life, which reckon nothing of human history or frantic need, but unfold, transform, and endure over billions of years. The Mystery of Regeneration is hidden, yet open, in this fusion of the 3rd, 2nd, and 9th Emanations of the Tree of Life.

This is the power of universal Understanding, the contraction and indrawing of Being, flowing back into the Void. It is the vessel within which All is contained, therefore within which All is comprehended. The Dark Mother or Great goddess is the deity of this 3rd Emanation, she who draws all unto herself.

2nd Emanation or sphere: Neptune, Wisdom, the Star Father

This is the power of universal Wisdom, the expansion of Being that flows in perfection out of the Void, towards increasing manifestation. Traditionally this sphere is associated with the primal father, the Star Father, the "male" polarity of outgoing, pattern making, Divine Consciousness. This is the Emanation that declares the universe. The utterance of the divine Name is the mystery of Wisdom. From the primal being at the Crown of the Tree of Life, a movement of expansion begins. This becomes the patterned Stars, whose energy and movement define the universe.

1st Emanation or sphere: Uranus, Crown of Stars

Uranus is the Crown of Being, the First Breath that flows out of the Void, and the Last Breath that returns to the Void. It is Being, Stillness, and Unity.

The Void

The Tree of Life is a sequence of interlaced Emanations that become increasingly manifest as both life forms and material substance. The Tree, the universe of Being, comes out of the Void, out of Unbeing. We cannot speculate upon the Void in text, but we can discover it in meditation. The Stillness form, in which we find the stillness of Unbeing within ourselves, is our way into the Void. Not a terrifying emptiness, but a realm of utter stillness and sacred potential.

Chapter 3

Angels, Archangels, and the Tree of Life

We cannot practice Qabalah without working with angels, archangels, and related spirits. All branches of all Tree of Life traditions affirm this to be so. In a modern demystified Qabalah, there is another way to state this truth. When we enter into our meditations, and use forms to change awareness and subtle energies, we are already working with the angels. Indeed, we are within them, and they are within us. We could not exist without this mutual interaction, between the angelic orders and ourselves. Practical Qabalah, spiritual magic, consists of opening our conscious awareness to their actions and their presence, regardless of any tradition in which we choose to work.

We should be aware that angels are present in any spiritual activity: we do not have to believe in them, name them, enumerate them, or even know that they exist any more than we have to know every organ of the body to digest a sandwich or take a walk. Most of the universe works perfectly well without human analysis, though we often forget this truth.

Angels and archangels are not gods and goddesses: deities are cultural and regional; they are the result of human experience, in particular lands, working with spiritual forces. Each deity has a further connection to cosmic forces and to greater deities within which they are subsumed. Yet, they are, so to speak, humanized through their intercourse with us. Angels are not humanized in this manner.

Regrettably, we live in an age when the idea of angels is ruthlessly trivialized and commercialized on one hand, or rendered intellectually obscure and unapproachable on the other. Any New Age or spiritual bookstore and gift shop abounds in examples of the first category of sentiment and commercialization, and usually has a few books that amply demonstrate the second category of intellectual complexity. We might, in the past, have been able to learn more about the traditions concerning angels from the orthodox religions, but the angelic aspects of Christianity, Islam, and Judaism, have been greatly downplayed in the 20th century, especially those of Christianity. Angelic traditions are preserved, however, in the mystical traditions within the three dogmatic religions.

One of our tasks in this book is to present, and work within, a direct and uncomplicated frame of reference for interaction between humans and angels. To do so, we must first explore the nature of angels as described in the perennial spiritual traditions that are at the foundation of religion and mysticism, and which have practical applications in working with the Miracle Tree. So, just what are angels?

Angels are the Messengers of the Divine Being

This is the one concept that all traditions and religions (that work with angels) agree upon: they are the Messengers of the Divine Being, of the universal consciousness.

As such, angels and archangels carry or relay the Word of Creation through the Three Worlds. Figure 2 on pg. 34 shows this classic model, which is widely applicable in meditation. *Angels are the carriers of consciousness between one state or condition and another.* In the original utterance of the universe, the movement was one way...from Unbeing to Being, from Being to manifestation: a movement of expansion. But a simultaneous movement of contraction occurs, in which forces move from manifestation towards and eventually into the Void of Unbeing. Angels move in both directions. This is the key to the traditional teaching that they carry both the Word of the Divine Being to the creation, and the prayers and aspirations of the created beings to the Divine Source.

As far as we are concerned on Earth, angels and archangels comprise three orders:

1. The angels of the Lunar World that are said, in Qabalistic tradition, to carry the thoughts and prayers of humanity and the responses of the Solar Being. This is a traditional teaching that emphasizes a human perspective: it applies equally to the consciousness of all living beings on Planet Earth, and to the planetary consciousness itself.

2. The angels of the Solar World carry the messages of the Solar Being and the responses of the other Stars. These "messages" are the interactions of consciousness and energy of the Sun and the solar system, in their ceaseless exchange with other Stars. The messages, or consciousness, of the Lunar World are included within this greater exchange.

3. The angels of the Stellar World carry the messages of the Stars, and the original Word of the Divine Being. The consciousness of the

Solar and Lunar Worlds is included within this universal exchange.

A human can, given sufficient training and clarity, ride on the consciousness of the angels of the Solar and Stellar Worlds. Many Qabalistic techniques of meditation and ritual depend upon this concept.

In Qabalistic tradition, the Tree of Life has 10 hosts of angels and 10 archangels: these exist within one another, just as the cells and organs of a human body exist within one another. A host of angels makes up the body of one archangel. The Ten, each made up of a host of angels like cells, are the organs of the body of One, the archangel that reaches from the Kingdom of Earth to the Crown of the Stars. This archangel, called Metatron in tradition, is the special patron of Qabalah. We will return to this tradition again, as it has major implications in practical work with the Tree of Life. This organic pattern of angels and archangels is implicit within the structure of the universal Tree of Life. The entire Tree is the pattern of the universe, and this entirety is mirrored in the relationship of the archangels wherein 10 comprise one.

In traditional Qabalah, we are taught that this archangel of archangels, Metatron, the Master of the Wings, contains, within its androgynous consciousness the prophet Enoch. This is a valuable, though somewhat obscure, teaching. Enoch, in Biblical terms, was the prophet who "walked with God and was not." He was literally taken up, bodily, into the divine consciousness. This tradition of holy men and women who vanish physically is found in many world traditions, of course, and is not limited to the Judaeo-Christian or Islamic streams. To simplify the entire story, it can be understood as a spiritual allegory, in which something of human consciousness is near to divine consciousness. Every man or woman has a fragment of this Enochian consciousness in them, and it is resonant of the great archangel that reaches from Earth to Heaven, who is said to *Proclaim before the Highest Throne*, at the Crown of the Tree of Life. But it is more than an allegory, for in Qabalah we work literally with the archangel Metatron, and with the prophetic consciousness that is at the very seat and throne of universal Being. In Jewish Qabalah, the prophet Enoch is a revered innerworld contact. In western Qabalah, the angelic "language" is often termed *Enochian*, based on the psychic experiments of the 16th century mathematician, astrologer, and cryptographer Dr. John Dee.[1] The *Book of Enoch* is a classic Qabalistic text, and can only be understood in a Qabalistic traditional context. Unfortunately, it has become the plaything of journalistic fancy in modern publication, simply because people who "discover" its reputed secrets have no Qabalistic background or training. Rather like someone who has never seen a car shrilly claiming to disclose the secrets of an engine maintenance manual.[2]

Whatever Happened to Angels?

The comfortable idea of the personalized humanocentric angel, so widespread today in this age of materialist reductionism, does not exist in the Qabalistic traditions. Indeed, it is a product of 19th century sentiment, and may be traced as such easily through art and literature. The New Age idea of angels, recently fashionable, is inherited directly from the Victorian era, strongly influenced by Spiritualism. Whatever the spirits are that work with New Age channelers or psychics, they are not angels. However, many inhabitants of the spirit worlds will masquerade as something in order to communicate or to get attention. We are fortunate that the older spiritual traditions (ranging from the Bible to the Koran to the mystical descriptions of

Qabalists, saints, and seers) are coherent and mutually confirm one another. Few of them have cozy humanoid angels who talk in endearing terms to us. Indeed, the traditional descriptions of angels are often strange, somewhat disturbing, and distinctly nonhuman. This disturbing or unsettling quality should not surprise us. Angels are an order of Life very different from humanity. They are vehicles of the creative and destructive forces of the Divine Being, the cosmic language of the Word. Traditionally, we are taught that angels exist regardless of humanity...but that humanity cannot exist regardless of angels.

The traditional definition of angels, which is also cultural, is often seen as poetic or allegorical: it has, of course, elements of dogma and propaganda within it, according to whichever religion you examine. But to the practical Qabalist, it is a simple statement of truth, describing *that which is so*. Angels carry or relay the Word, which contains within Itself the creative and destructive impulses of the universe. Thus they are Messengers, Carriers, Proclaimers, and Disseminators. All of these words, by the way, are found as angelic names or names of angelic hosts in the Hebrew and Arabic names of the angels. In other words, *the names describe the functions*. This is important for us. *Angels do things*. If we are able to attune to what they carry, what they communicate, what they do, it can, and will, transform us.

Angels arose before humans out of the Void...they are of the power-foundation of the universe, linking the shapes and forces of the Word, of the Creation. Indeed, the Word of Creation, which carries both creative and destructive forces within it, is the source of the angels. They are, to use the sound analogy further, the harmonics or partials of the Word. The Word itself is vast as the universe, but the angels proclaim distinct parts of it. Thus they are the Messengers.

An abstract musical analogy is used frequently in Qabalah, especially those variants that come to us from the Neo-Platonic and Pythagorean traditions. This idea of resonance and harmony, of harmonics and sound waves, is directly related to the "advanced" worldview of modern mathematical physics. Indeed, angels live in such abstract dimensions, for they are in the places in between the manifest worlds, linking such worlds together through their utterance, resonance, and harmony. The late Dion Fortune, writing in her book *Applied Magic*[3] says:

> *It is said by the rabbis that these beings are perfect, each after their own kind; but they do not evolve, and it is noticeable that they are non-intellectual. One might almost call them divine Robots each strictly conditioned by its own nature perfectly to fulfill the office for which it was created; free from all struggle and inner conflict, but changeless, and therefore unevolving.*

Archangels Especially Associated with Our World

There are four archangels that have a special connection to our Planet Earth, and have long been associated with Qabalah, magical arts, and the spiritual forces of human development. They are found in the 6th, 7th, 8th, and 9th Emanations (*see figure 1*). These are often called the four great archangels, and are further associated with the planetary directions of East, South, West, and North (*see figure 7*). All archangels are androgynous, being before male/female polarity. A remnant of this important teaching, long preserved in Qabalistic tradition, is found in the many icons of the archangels, in which they are obviously male figures with a feminine quality.

Archangel Michael

In the 6th Emanation, the sphere of Harmony, the archangel of the Sun is Michael. This archangel holds in Balance the creative and destructive forces of our Star. Thus it is the archangel of Light that protects and purifies, and its presence disposes of imbalances and disharmony. Michael is associated with the direction South, the element of Fire, and the times of midsummer and midday. Michael works with the staff or spear of balance, the rod of direction. The key concept for Michael is Light.

Archangel Auriel

In the 7th Emanation, the sphere of Exaltation, the archangel of Venus is Auriel. This archangel reflects and raises up the powers of manifestation, and ministers Grace. Auriel is the archangel of force shaping into form, and brings insight and experience through the forces of attraction and interaction. The direction of Auriel is the North, the element is Earth, and the times are midwinter and midnight. Auriel works with the shield or mirror, the surface of form. The key concept for Auriel is Law.

Archangel Raphael

In the 8th Emanation, the sphere of Brilliance, the archangel of Mercury is Raphael. This archangel inspires and instructs, and is also the keeper of honorable power wielded with integrity. Raphael is the archangel of healing arts and the sciences. The direction of Raphael is the East, and the element is Air. Raphael works with the sword or arrow, and, more specifically, with the point or fine edge of form, where it disperses into energy. The key concept for Raphael is Life.

Archangel Gabriel

In the 9th Emanation, the sphere of Foundation, the archangel of the Moon is Gabriel. This archangel mediates compassion, creative fertility, and the spiritual forces of generation and regeneration. Gabriel is the archangel of the oceans, of ebbing and flowing tides. The direction of Gabriel is the West, and the element is Water. Gabriel works with the cup or vessel, that which contains gives forth, and sustains. The key concept for Gabriel is Love.

A standard and highly effective meditation with the Four archangels is to sense them around you: Raphael before you, Michael to your right, Auriel to your left, and Gabriel behind you. Do this while facing east. When you have practiced this simple form, you can face each direction in turn, experiencing each archangel in each of the four relative places.

Working with Angels

The good news is that we are already working with angels, relating to them, interacting with them. Without such interaction we would cease to exist, cease to have life or form. However, due to the consciousness-phenomenon called the Abyss, we find ourselves to be separate from the angels. In a universal sense, the Abyss is the infinite extent of Time, Space, and Energy between the Stars. More specifically, it is the distance between our Sun, and any other Star. This distance has its imprint in our consciousness. When we die, and when we are born, we cross the Abyss between death and rebirth. When we sleep, we cross the lesser Abyss between two modes of consciousness, between waking and sleeping.

The key to understanding this phenomenon is linked to memory. We forget that which we are, and thus we become separated from our true selves, and so we become separated from the angels. The human consciousness reiterates the creation process, of progressive externalization or manifestation. This process, of expansion, creates the abyss of time and space within which cosmic forces flow (nowadays much studied by physicists and astronomers, but originally explored by Qabalists, who laid the foundations for modern science during the Renaissance in Europe). In our day-to-day thoughts, it leads to exclusion and forgetting.

Bridging the Abyss

Any forms that will help us relate to angelic consciousness are forms that cross the abyss within consciousness, that build bridges between the conditioned outer personality and the eternal inner spirit that comes into many lives, not merely one. Bridge building is an ancient Qabalistic exercise, and the sword-bridge, bridge of ice and Fire, or single strand of cord over the abyss, are found in many spiritual myths and legends worldwide. When we begin bridge building, there are specific orders of angels that work with us. Thus, we are not alone in this spiritual task. Indeed, one of the inherent abilities of humanity is to *connect*, to build bridges. Great spiritual teachers and mythic kings are associated with this ability, and to this day the head of the Catholic Church is called *pontiff*, a title taken outright from the *pontifex* or High Priest of ancient Rome. Pontifex means bridge maker, from the root *pons*, a bridge.

Humanity bridges between the gods and goddesses and the manifest world, and between the angels and the world of living beings in nature. As bridge building is one of our inherent skills, let us go to it.

The Bridge Building Form: Part 1

This form begins as a typical visualized scenario, which you undertake while sitting with a candle upon a stand or small altar in front of you. Once you have practiced it and built your bridge, you will be able to enter it immediately without the detailed narrative. In stage two, the form is done standing, without the candle, and involves movement.

The following narrative should be used repeatedly until you are able to build and cross the bridge without it. As we have angelic assistance with this task, you may be surprised how rapidly the bridge is built.

1. Be Still. Use the Stillness Form.
2. Light a single candle, and recite The Litany of The Flame aloud:

Behold the Terrestrial Fire that comes from the center of the Earth. The Terrestrial Fire is an embodiment of the Celestial Fire. It is both Sun and Stars present within Earth and manifest upon the Altar. Wherever the Light of the Flame is reflected from substance, it is the Lunar Fire. Stars, Sun, and Moon, all live within in this Flame, shed their Light upon us, and radiate within us.

3. Meditate on the flame, which embodies all Being, and for us on Earth, is the living flame of the 3 Suns (*see Chapter 6*).
4. Look through and beyond the flame. On the other side, build a strong image of a simple arched bridge. It can be of stone, wood, glass, or any substance you choose. A rainbow bridge, the bridge of Promise, or a bridge of Light is used in traditional Qabalah. Sometimes it will manifest to your inner vision in a specific way. If this happens, work with that

manifestation, for it is your "hallmark" vision of the bridge. Traditionally the bridge is shining with the inner Light that crosses the Abyss.

5. Sit and calmly build the image of the Bridge. Let your awareness rest upon it. If your awareness strays, return to the bridge. Do not strain or sweat at this, do it gently, but firmly.

6. Meditate on the qualities of "bridging." What does a bridge do? How does it work? What happens when we cross a bridge? What happens when we return? What is under the bridge? What is over it? Gradually condense these bridge-streams of consciousness down into a wordless feeling of *bridge-ness*. Be Still, communing with the essence of the Bridge on the other side of the Flame. (Do not cross the Bridge at this time).

7. Return to your outer awareness, draw back from the bridge communion. Affirm the four cardinal directions, sky above, land below. Put out the flame. (Make notes or keep a journal if you wish.)

Notes on developing Part 1 of the Bridge Building Form

Repeat this visualization until the bridge starts to appear rapidly of its own accord. This will not take long, as this form is hallowed by ancient tradition, and has enormous energy behind it. Furthermore, by building the vision-bridge, you are creating conditions of consciousness and energy whereby angelic beings will recognize your intent and work with you. When the bridge becomes clear each time, you should progress to the second stage of the form.

The Bridge Building Form: Part 2

1. Repeat parts 1-6 of the first stage of this form.

7. While sitting, see, sense, and feel yourself stepping onto the bridge. To do so, you pass through the flame.

8. Pause on the bridge, and form your awareness of the Directions. Before you is the bridge across the Abyss. Behind you is the human world. To your right and left you will gradually sense and feel angelic presences. These are the angels of grace that attend us at birth and at death, and whenever we cross to and fro into the spiritual dimensions during life. Traditionally, they are invisible beings that support us, that strengthen and uphold us. As you pause on the bridge, reach out and feel for their presence. They will respond and draw close: often you will "see" nothing, but you will feel them on either side.

9. Be Still. Commune wordlessly with the angelic presences that support you. Exchange with them. You may see images; you may feel subtle forces flowing through your body. Be calm, and commune in peace.

10. In your enhanced visualization, acknowledge the angelic presence, and slowly step (backwards) from the bridge, and backwards through the flame. You may feel a force, rather like suction or a sticky sensation as you do so. Now you are back in the human world. Become aware of yourself in your meditation chair again, or sitting on the floor, whichever way you work. Close by being aware of the directions, sky, and land. Use the Crossing Form (*see Chapter 6*).

Notes on part 2 of the Bridge Building Form

Work with this until you have clear sense of the angelic supporters at the threshold of the bridge. Usually this only takes three sessions to establish, though in some cases it happens spontaneously, and in others it takes further practice. But it always happens, because it is a working model of a state of Being, of something that really is there: a bridge that we cross too seldom. When the angels come to you as you step onto the bridge, you are ready to cross. This is stage three.

The Bridge Building Form: Part 3

Complete stages 1-10. Cross the bridge. What is on the other side? When you return, write an account of what happened.

Notes on Part 3 of the Bridge Building Form

Make this unconditional crossing frequently. With practice, the entire form can be condensed into a five-minute meditation. Working through the three stages described above and following the gradual pattern of progress will lead rapidly to your natural, inherent, bridge-building ability.

The Bridge Building Form: Part 4

The next stage is to cross the bridge to specific locations. Many Qabalists use this method to enter into the qualities or consciousness and energy of the 10 Emanations. You are in the 10th sphere, and you cross to the 9th, and so forth. Work with this simple pattern; use the illustration (*see figure 1, pg. 33*). Some students map out a Tree of Life on the floor, and literally walk throughout, combining this physical movement with the bridge making and crossing.

However, the older form, and by far the most powerful, is to work with the Paths of the Tree. The Paths are explored in Chapter 7, but before working with them, you should develop through the forms described in the interim chapters.

Chapter 4

Returning to Eden

In this chapter, you will discover how to work with three powerfully transformative forms, each based on the Tree of Life.

The Garden of Eden: a set of interrelated forms, which combine to make a greater or hyper-form. This set is a complete Qabalah in itself, and could be the basis for long-term practice. In essence, it is an alternative way of working with the Tree of Life, without using any of the detailed structure of Emanations or Paths. They are all inherent in the Garden.

Breathing A Room: a form for indoor use, which, like the first form, is an alternative way of working with the Tree of Life without Emanations or Paths. Once you have practiced this form, you can work with Emanations and Paths within it, if you wish to combine them.

The Qabalah of Three Suns: a unique form that works with the stellar, solar, and planetary forces within the body. This is another complete Qabalah, stripping away all the attributes and use of imagery. It works only with the primary entities of the three Suns, Above, Below, and Within.

Once you have spent some time working with these forms, you will discover that they have many connections, yet they work in very different ways. The progression from The Garden of Eden to The Qabalah of Three Suns involves a continued simplification of your Tree of Life experience, from the more complex Garden of Eden set, to the spiritual properties of shape explored in Breathing a Room, to the essence of spiritual force, in the Three Suns.

Some students might say, "Why don't we cut straight to Three Suns, then?" For practical work, I would recommend doing all three sets of forms in order. In Qabalistic practice, you do not outgrow a form or a discipline: it changes you. When you return to what seemed at first to be a basic practice, or perhaps a difficult or complex practice, it will work for you in a new way. We change, but the forms are constant: constant and open to infinite effects. This is one of the secrets of Qabalah that are available for anyone willing to work with the Tree of Life. *Meditating upon this secret of the forms and practices is deeply rewarding.*

The Garden of Eden

One of the primary spiritual legends associated with the Tree of Life is that of the Garden. In the religions of the Book (Judaism, Christianity, Islam), it is known as the Garden of Eden, drawing on a theme taken from Babylonian myth. According to legend, the Garden is said to be at Al Qrnah, in what is now Iraq, at the confluence of the Tigris and Euphrates rivers, in what used to be Mesopotamia. But the Garden has many other antecedents, and is the core of many myths worldwide. The politics of religion has given the Middle Eastern legend an exaggerated role as the "original." In truth, the original Garden is not in any religion, nor is it in our consensual or conditioned outer world, but can be rediscovered in the spiritual realms out of which this world is shaped. Once we have rediscovered the primal Garden, we will have the Knowledge to transform the outer world according to its image.

The theme of a primal garden land is found in Plato with the legend of Atlantis; in Hesiod, with the legend of the Golden Age; and in Celtic tradition with the legend of the Fortunate Isles.[1] Many more examples could be cited, but the four listed above have direct connections to the fusion of spiritual traditions that we call Qabalah today.

If you wish to know more about the early sources, you will find ample reference material in the texts cited in the footnotes. In this chapter, we are going explore the spiritual and transformative implications of the Tree and Garden legend, and discover how we may apply them in life today.

The Tree and Garden legend

All variants of the legend have two or three things in common: a tree, a spring, and a fruitful land, garden, or island. Sometimes the tree is associated with the spring; sometimes the spring or the tree is found alone, but either spring or tree (or both) is located within a primal land, garden, or island. In ancient Scottish faery tradition, the Tree is found in the Underworld where it grows at the Crossroads of the Hidden Ways, as described in the ancient magical ballad of Thomas Rhymer, and in the longer 13th century Romance poem also associated with Rhymer.[2] In the Welsh bardic Merlin legends (as formalized into Latin by Geoffrey of Monmouth 12th century C.E.) replete with Qabalistic elements, the Fortunate Isles produce all good things and are ruled by a goddess with her nine sisters. These nine sister-goddesses from Celtic mythology, like the Muses of classical tradition, embody the Tree of Life, with its nine Emanations (3x3), which manifest as a 10th, the garden or island, or world. In an ancient Greek text, by Hesiod, the benevolent titan Cronos rules the garden island of the Hesperides: the sacred tree produces golden apples. The associated legend of Jason and the Golden Fleece describes an island paradise, with a sacred tree upon which the fleece is hung.[3] In the works of Plato, the benevolent titan is Atlas, who founds a shrine at a sacred spring in the center of a fertile island. From this source the first civilization grows and becomes the lost culture of Atlantis.

In the Garden of Eden legend, a tree grows in the center of a natural paradise, and four rivers (from a spring at the roots of the tree) flow out to the four directions of East, South, West, and North. This simple form is the basis of the tradition, and has many practical applications. Gradually, as we know, each variant of the legend describes how humanity becomes separated from the Garden, and becomes imbalanced and corrupt.

According to Plato, who draws upon a tradition at the roots of Western Qabalah, a vast powerful civilization develops, and is eventually destroyed by cataclysm. This legend of Atlantis is at the core of the esoteric tradition of the West, though the reader should be cautious, as almost all contemporary texts on Atlantis are fabrications based on 19th century material by the Theosophical Society. When in doubt, work only with the primary legends from original sources, and there you will discover the pattern that is the progenitor of all the later stories.

In the Judaeo-Christian traditions, Adam and Eve are expelled for eating of the fruit of the Tree of Knowledge (Knowledge of Good and Evil, a theme that has been heavily propagandized and misrepresented). While the legend found in Plato deals with planetary forces of growth, civilization, and cataclysm in the Atlantic zone, the legend of Adam and Eve is at a primal level, dealing with human spiritual manifestation. Both tell the same story, but at different stages, and in different modes. In other words, human civilization, and humanity itself, repeats an inherent pattern that arose within our primal ancestors. This primal pattern is rooted in the forces of universal creation and manifestation. The ideas of dualistic "good and evil" and "original sin" are propagandist elements woven into the legend at a later date: they form the ground into which many of the ills of our culture were seeded, ills which still flourish strongly today in mutated forms within obsessive materialism and compulsive modernism.

One of the most significant Qabalistic practices has always been to use the legend of the Garden, the Tree, and Adam and Eve, as a way back to the Garden. As the journey of the primal parents out of the Garden has been well mapped by texts and by oral tradition, we may retrace their footsteps back into that primal realm, where the spring rises at the roots of the Tree of Life. This simple proposition has been part of the "secret" tradition within Qabalah for many centuries, and there is a range of techniques arising from its practical application. They vary from celibate mysticism to sexual ritual magic, but all have the same aim, to retrace the steps of the primal humans back to central tree, spring, and garden, that are at the heart of all creation. In Appendix D, you will find a legend from the mystical Grail Tradition, from a medieval source, that is one of the early texts describing the secret methods of returning to the Garden. A variant of this legend became the basis for Ethiopian or Salomonic Qabalah, a significant branch of the tradition that has been ignored by Western Qabalists for too long.

At the heart of all the legends, therefore, are two powerful concepts. The first is that these are true and valuable accounts of events in spiritual dimensions, associated with the process of creation and manifestation, with the externalization of humanity into the Kingdom. The second is that we may use these legends (any of them, from any branch of the tradition) to retrace our steps, and come back into the Garden. To do this, we have to work with versions of the legendary sequence that are empowered by the inner tradition, as well as founded in the outer. Here are some forms that will enable your return.

The Eden Forms

The Eden forms are interconnected, and make a set of exercises that have a long-term effect upon consciousness. Like many branches of the Tradition, these forms comprise a complete Qabalah in themselves, and can be practiced without reference to any other methods. However, the Qabalist should be informed, educated, and practiced in all aspects of the tradition that comes from the Tree of Life. In practical terms, as stated throughout this book, the forms described in each chapter interact with one another, and mutually strengthen one another.

There are four Eden forms: The Four Rivers, Rootedness, Becoming Adam and Eve, and Becoming the Tree of Life.

Each of these four forms should be practiced in order. Work through them one by one, becoming familiar with each form before you begin the next. As your participation in the forms develops and intensifies, they will merge into one another, and eventually you will be able to participate in all four as one, during the fourth form, *Becoming the Tree of Life*. Do not rush this process: it is one of realignment of consciousness and energy at first, and with practice it becomes an organic development of spiritual transformation. To put it more simply, these are four steps towards the Garden—take them one at a time.

As mentioned above, the four Eden forms comprise a complete Qabalah in their own right, and could be your main practice for a lifetime. A working Qabalist often tries a number of forms and branches of the tradition, before settling for those forms that work most powerful for him or her in this lifetime. Be cautious with this idea, for it is not about dabbling. It implies serious, deep work within the tradition and gradually working through certain forms to come out on the other side of them. From that Other Side (beyond and liberated from conditioned consensual consciousness), the same forms are found to work in new ways. The forms remain true unto themselves, but we change through our interaction with the forms. Therefore one form or one set of forms will work in many ways for us, and can never be "used up" or "outgrown." On the Tree of Life, the most advanced spiritual exercises and realizations are identical to those at the beginning of your journey. This is only a paradox when we have not tried the Paths of the Tree, and it resolves itself as we work within the tradition.

Practicing the Eden Forms

Before practicing these four forms, use a compass or some other accurate means to discover where North is, relative to your position. The alignment of the Four Directions is important in all Tree of Life work, as the planetary forces greatly enhance your inner work. In forms of this sort, East is often before you, though you may, of course, work facing any of the four directions. In later forms, the directions become more specified, with emphasis on the polarized forces of each. Consult Figure 7, The Universal Map, on page 39 before practicing the Eden forms.

You may work with these forms in three ways:

1. *Work with what is there*. Discover and work with the natural features of each direction. Know where the oceans, the mountains, the forest, or any major natural features stand in relation to where you stand.

2. *Work with the Primal Map*, attuning to the Four Elements and Four Powers, as shown on the map. Once you have familiarized yourself with both step 1 and 2, you will easily move on to:

3. *Merging steps 1 and 2* so that you work with the features of land and sea around you, attuning with them, and through them, to the elements and powers of the Primal Map. Never forget to work with the land where you are: Qabalah and Tree of Life work should not be practiced only in a theoretical space, but must always relate to the living land and Planet. Most of the confusions of literary Qabalah will disappear when you come out of theoretical abstract space into a relationship with the land and Planet. How could it be otherwise?

1st Eden Form: The Four Rivers

1. Begin by being still, stilling Time, Space, and Movement, using the Stillness form described in Chapter 2. Be aware of the sky above and the land below. Be aware of the direction before you, the direction behind you, and those on your right and left. The direction before you (usually East or West) flows to you; the direction behind you flows through you; those on your right and left strengthen and uphold

you between above and below. Thus you are balanced at the center of the four directions, with sky above and land below.

2. See before you the shining river of the East (West). It flows from your feet, beginning as a small stream, then widening into a mighty river that extends to the horizon. Let your awareness pass along this river: sense, see, and feel where it flows, and what forces flow within it.

3. See behind you the shining river of the West (East). It flows from your feet, beginning as a small stream, then widening into a mighty river that extends to the horizon. Let your awareness pass along this river: sense, see, and feel where it flows, and what forces flow within it.

4. See to your right the shining river of the South (North). It flows from your feet, beginning as a small stream, then widening into a mighty river that extends to the horizon. Let your awareness pass along this river: sense, see and feel where it flows, and what forces flow within it.

5. See to your left the shining river of the North (South). It flows from your feet, beginning as a small stream, then widening into a mighty river that extends to the horizon. Let your awareness pass along this river: sense, see, and feel where it flows, and what forces flow within it.

6. Rest in the awareness that you are eternally at the source of the Four Rivers. Encompass them within you; flow out with them to the horizons of the world. Flow back into yourself, and be still.

7. Close your awareness of the Four Rivers, one by one. East, West, South, North. Sense again the sky above, the land below. Return to your outer awareness.

Notes on practicing the Four Rivers Form

This is a standing form, and is best undertaken with eyes open. It is not a withdrawn or entranced visualization. Ideally it should be done outdoors, somewhere quiet, where you can stand without distraction or interruption. As a second choice, it can be practiced indoors, standing. The Four Rivers form is greatly enabled and enhanced by regular work with the Walking Participation form, but you should not combine the two forms. The Four Rivers is a standing-still, visible form, while Walking Participation is a mobile, invisible form. Visible forms are those that are obvious to an observer as some kind of special practice, while invisible forms can be done in the midst of daily life without obvious signs that they are special practices.

There are three stages to your development within the form:

1st stage: Build each River one at a time. Do not attempt to work with all Four immediately. If you wish, you can train in this form by spending a few minutes on only one River, then closing. Simply leave out the sections for the other three, but follow the rest of the pattern described above. Work next on two Rivers, one before you, and one behind you. Stay with this until you are familiar with them, and then proceed to the 3rd and 4th rivers, those of right and left.

2nd stage: Once you are familiar with the form, build all Rivers sequentially: before you, behind you, right, and left. This is the essence of the form, so work toward this, and practice it frequently. With practice, you will be able to open out the Rivers sequentially or simultaneously, though opening them sequentially is recommended.

3rd stage: Breathing. Once you have the Four Rivers established, this form uses a breathing rhythm. On your in-breath, sense the rivers flowing to you: on your out-breath, sense them flowing away from you. Your breath should be steady, deep, and rhythmic. Let the flow of breath be natural, and do not fall into any other breathing exercises that you may already know. Work only with the rhythm of the breath, and the flowing of the Rivers.

Opening and Closing Forms

Always begin and end by entering Silence, stilling Time, Space, and Movement. Use the Stillness form. This is our human participation in the universal event of Being emanating from the Void of Unbeing. From Stillness, affirm the sky above, land below, and the four directions. You can also use the Qabalistic "crossing" formula that is found in Chapter 6 to open and close all workings and forms.

2nd Eden Form: Rootedness

This is a variant of the primary Rising Light form, and when you have practiced the Rising Light, you will be able to progress to this form easily.

1. Stand and affirm the Seven Directions.
2. Go into Stillness, stilling Time, Space, and Movement.
3. Let your awareness descend down your body to the soles of your feet. Sense and feel that you have roots, reaching deep down into the body of the Land, into the heart of the Planet. These roots are tree-like, proliferating in many directions through the body of the land. Sense and feel your Rootedness.

4. Spend time building this sense of Rootedness, and rest within it. In this form, you do not encourage the Earth Light or subtle energies to rise (as in the Rising Light form), though you may find that they do so spontaneously. If this happens, feel the Earth Light circulating in your body, and let it return back down into the roots. This cycle is a natural, tidal pattern and will establish itself without strenuous effort.

5. Practice the form in various places: indoors, outdoors, at different locations. Be aware that your Rootedness is not dependent on any one place. At first, build the form while standing still. Next, work with it while walking.

6. When you walk, be aware of your Rootedness. As you raise your feet, you will sense "stickiness," as the roots rise momentarily. This stickiness occurs with all things that we touch or connect to, both physically and subtly. We have many "sticky" connections to the past, to ancestral lands, to places and people. Most of the time we are not aware of them, though they become obvious when we are connected to loved ones. By loosening and rendering our roots elastic, we free up subtle forces that flow between the Earth and us and build an organic network of connections.

Most people need to reconnect to their roots before they can experience the elasticity of walking while in Rootedness. In the older Qabalistic practices the emphasis was upon loosening the sticky web of connections, making it flexible, and realigning it. Before we can do this, however, we have to become aware of the web of connections, which is done through our feelings, through a subtle sense of touch connected with the element of Earth within us. In the Eden legend, the Adam (or primal androgynous human) has a body made of Earth. This is one of the esoteric clues to working with the Foundations of our spiritual Being through the body. The disconnection of our contemporary human culture, based on denial of and aggression towards the world of nature, takes many forms. Working with Rootedness will free us from these restrictions, literally step by step, as we walk within the form.

7. Once you have developed the form standing and walking, and have rendered your roots elastic and pliable, you can move on to the next phase of Rootedness. This involves working with the Primal Map, and is done standing. Later you may work with this stage while walking.

    Find yourself at the center of the Seven Directions, and be Still. Open your awareness of Rootedness. Feel your roots reaching out to each of the four directions in turn, until they are extended to the four cardinal points of East, South, West, and North.

    At first this will seem a flat pattern, but as your roots extend, be aware that they curve around the Planet, extending to the directions, then delving downwards at the horizons of the directions.

    The roots curve around and join together Beneath, and then rise as one into the trunk of your body through the soles of your feet.

8. When you have practiced step 7, work with the root forces flowing the other way, with roots extending directly down from your feet, deep into the center of the Planet. From there they curve upwards to each of the four cardinal

directions, and reach back into your feet from
before you, behind, to right, and left.

3rd Eden Form: Becoming Adam and Eve

Before we begin with this form, we should clarify
some of the gender themes that have constellated around
the myth. We are not working with a patriarchal male-
orientated tradition here, but with the inner tradition,
which has always been known to practicing Qabalists. The
hidden aspects of this tradition were preserved in many
ways, such as the story in Appendix D, but mostly by oral
teaching. The primal Adam, sometimes called Adam
Cadmon from Jewish tradition, is an androgynous being.
This primal Adam has a prototypical presence throughout
the universe, and takes form as planetary life, on any Planet.

In our world of Earth, the primal Adam becomes the
human race. The myth of woman created from man's rib
was originally one of polarization, of spiritual humanity
dividing from androgyny towards polarity. This is shown
in the tarot trump of the Lovers, where a veiled figure
radiates blessing towards man and woman, who are about
to travel separate Paths. To become Adam and Eve, we
must recover our inner sense of androgyny. No man or
woman is totally male or totally female…such a being would
be a terrible monster. That is why, of course, we find the
exaggerated stereotypes of the all-male or the all-woman
so absurd.

Here is the form, Becoming Adam and Eve:

1. Enter Stillness. Affirm the Seven Directions
    (Above, Below, Before, Behind, Right, Left,
    Within). Align yourself to the planetary
    directions, with East before you.
2. Be aware of your Right and Left. On your
    right, see, sense and feel the primal woman

as a pure being of spiritual essence. On your
left, see, sense and feel the primal man as a
pure being of spiritual essence.

3. Let the feminine aspects of yourself flow out
into the primal woman to your right. Let the
masculine aspects of yourself flow into the
primal man on your left.

4. Be Still at the center. Rest awhile in peace
and stillness, with this sense of the primal man
and woman on either side.

5. Begin to breathe deeply and steadily, pausing
momentarily at the end of each in-drawing and
out-going breath. At first simply breathe in,
pause, breathe out, pause. As you do this, the
primal man and woman will begin to breathe
with you.

6. When this mutual breathing is established, it
will begin to circulate between the "you" in
the center, and the primal Adam and Eve to
your left and right.

7. Gradually the primal Adam and Even merge
with you, slowly moving into you with the circulating pattern of breath.

8. Be Still, and be at One with the Adam and
the Eve partaking of themselves within you,
and you within them.

9. Affirm the Sky Above, the Land Below, and
the Four Directions. The Seventh Direction
is within, where the primal Adam and Eve are
at one within you.

10. Return to your outer awareness. Use the
Crossing formula.

Notes on Becoming Adam and Eve

1. During step 2 you may find that the primal man and woman are on the opposite sides to those described. If this happens, go with it. If at any time they change sides, after being fixed for a while, let this happen. There is an inner polarity and rhythm in this form that asserts itself spontaneously. Allow this to happen, and work with it. If, however, there is some uncertainty at the beginning, work with it exactly as described, until the form has built up energy. Do not concern yourself if they do not switch sides: just go with whatever happens between right and left.

2. In the early stages this form builds *simulacra* or psychic images of the pure man and woman forms. You may feel some loss of vital energy, though this is not inevitable, but more of an individual tendency. However, these simulacra hold within them the seeds of spirit, and they are not empty shells. Once you have worked steadily with the form, the primal spiritual forces that they embody so to speak, replace the simulacra. Any loss of vitality is replaced many fold. Then they merge as one, *within your own physical body.*

3. Some students of this form will find that it arouses sexual desire. This should not be surprising or a source of concern, as we are working with the male/female powers at an ever deepening level when we undertake the form. If you are aroused (regardless of your gender or sexual preference) continue with the entire sequence, and do not ground it

through physical scx. At stage 10 you will come into a sense of well-being and vitality. Then, of course, you may make Love!

4. For those who are not aroused sexually, the forces will still be flowing. By stage 10, you will also come into a sense of well-being and vitality.

5. In traditional Qabalah, the polarity forms are often combined with a phase of celibacy. As they are, essentially, sexual magic, it is important not to let the forces be repeatedly grounded. You should experience this form both with and without physical sex. If you live with a partner, you could practice the form together. However, it is not appropriate, and not recommended, that you persuade an unwilling partner to participate. If your partner is not interested in the practices, do not impose them upon him or her.

4th Eden Form: Becoming the Tree of Life

The fourth form is known in many variants as a "stand alone" meditation, a classic of Qabalistic practice. However, if you slowly build your forces through the Eden forms, and then work with the variant presented here, you will find it extremely powerful. Much of the literature on the Tree of Life is incomplete, either because the writers have no knowledge of the actual practices, or because the practices were completed by oral instruction. The absence of roots, for example, is widespread in texts and meditations on the Tree of Life. The Garden of Eden has a Tree with Roots, Adam and Eve at One, and the Four Rivers to water the world. Would you settle for less? With this fourth

Eden form, you will be working with a rich and potent interaction of the forms, so train up to it slowly, step by step.

1. Be Still. Affirm the Seven Directions.

2. Open to the Four Rivers.

3. Open to your Rootedness.

4. Become Adam and Eve, Eve and Adam.

5. Direct your awareness to your roots. Feel the Earth forces rising through them into your body.

6. Be aware that your Feet are in the Earth, your Genitals in the Moon, your heart in the Sun, your Head in the Stars.

7. Raise your Right hand upwards, palm open, above your head. This is the Hand of Severity. Raise your Left hand upwards, palm open, above your head. This is the Hand of Mercy.

8. Become the Tree of Life, with your roots in the Earth, your Crown in the Stars, your Right and Left branches reaching up in perfect Balance.

9. Sense, see, and feel the spiritual power that descends from the Stars to the Sun to the Moon, to the Earth. It flows down through the Tree, through your body. Be Still, and commune with the circulating powers, from Below to Above, from Above to Below. You are the primal Eve/Adam, within and of the Tree of Life, at the center of all Being.

10. Affirm the planetary directions, with your sense of the Rivers. Let the spiritual forces flow out unconditionally to the directions, along the Rivers. Use the Crossing form, and return to your outer awareness.

A Variant Hand Position of the Tree of Life Form

One of the traditional hand positions is with one hand palm open upraised to Heaven, and the other palm open (upwards) extended down to Earth. Try this variant after you have practiced the overall form. When you do this, one hand draws down from Heaven, while the other disperses to Earth. Meditate on this variant of the form, as it has many practical implications.

Breathing a room

This is an indoor form, related to the magical and philosophical concept of the Cube of Space. In metaphysics, magical geometry, and cosmology, the primary directions of space (above, below, before/east, behind/west, right/south, left/north) were formalized as a cube in meditation. This cube of space was conceived inside the sphere of Being.[4] All of this may seem rather abstract until we discover that far from being a mental exercise, the cube inside the sphere is a powerful tool for changing consciousness and energy. There is one proviso: you must shape it around you, not merely think about it or examine it in a diagram. All interaction with the Tree of Life must be lived to the fullest. Playing with proportions and attributes in Qabalah does little, but living within the realities that are indicated by such proportions or attributes will change us forever.

One of the simplest practical methods is to use an existing cube...this is why ancient temples, shrines, and esoteric lodges often had cubic proportions. But be aware, merely sitting inside a cube will do very little. You must interact consciously with the cosmic principles that the manifest cube embodies. After all, you do not merely sit in your parked car to go somewhere: you interact with it, and go through a travel process that begins with the first thought of the journey, but ends when the actual physical movement ceases. The manifest world mirrors the spiritual world, and certain principles apply throughout.

The cube and other defined shapes within a sphere (known in philosophy as the Platonic Solids) were used as vehicles to move awareness, to transport our Living Spirit into other dimensions of Being. They still work today, though the art has been much neglected. How could they not work? They are aspects of reality, of the universal pattern-making Being within which we all have our Being.

First find your Cube

The best cube that you have available is a room. If it is not perfectly square, simply work with its four sides, ceiling, and roof. The *Breathing a Room* form has many practical applications. Once you have practiced this form, you will find that the more abstract cube of space meditations are much easier, should you choose to do them, and your understanding of the (often obscure) texts on this subject will be greatly deepened. The abstract cube meditations are not aligned to a physical room or structure, but are sculpted in the space and time around you.

Breathing a Room

Choose a room that is regular and simple in shape, such as rectangular or square. It must present four walls, one in each direction. Small insets or alcoves for doors or closets make no difference, but do not practice this form in an irregularly shaped room. The properties of Shape are significant in all magical and spiritual work. Traditionally it is the 90 degree angle of the corners and the straight walls, floor, and ceiling that are more important than measuring the length or breadth. So you can use a long room, providing the angles of the walls are right angles. In simple practice, do not nit-pick over the proportions, and simply work as if it is a cube.

1. Stand in the center of the room, facing the wall that corresponds most closely with the planetary direction East. Understand this to be East. Therefore you have West behind you, and South and North to your right and left respectively. Be aware of the ceiling above, and the floor below. Spend a few moments *feeling* the room. Usually we think of rooms in terms of the activity that we do within them (the lounge, the bedroom, the office). In this Qabalistic form, the room becomes the theatre for spiritual activity, working not with its contents or daily-designated function, but with its primary shape. So feel the room, feel its six surfaces or faces. Feel yourself inside those six faces, seething with potential. Be still.

2. Enter into the Stillness form. Find yourself at the center of the room, in Silence.

3. *With eyes open*, breathe in, and gently blow your breath towards the east wall: feel your breath reaching out and billowing over the entire wall. Let the physical wall be filled with universal Life. Do this three times.

4. Turn to face the south wall. Repeat the breathing. Let the physical wall be filled with universal Light.

5. Turn to face the west wall. Repeat the breathing. Let the physical wall be filled with universal Love.

6. Turn to face the north wall. Repeat the breathing. Let the physical wall be filled with universal Law.

7. Look upwards to the ceiling. Repeat the triple breathing. Let the physical ceiling be filled with the power of the Stars Above.

8. Look downward to the floor. Repeat the triple breathing. Let the physical floor be filled with the power of the UnderWorld Below.

9. Be still in the center, breathing steadily. Feel your body at the center of the room. You are connected to the entire room by your feet on the floor, and by the triple breathing for each face of the room. Meditate in silence.

10. Close the form by facing each direction briefly, and seeing the wall in its outer form, its daily shape, and presentation. Finish with the ceiling and floor, and with your sense of the entire building connecting to the sky and land, above and below.

Optional variant: you can use the Crossing form on each face of the room, for opening and closing.

Notes on Breathing a Room

1. Choose a simple room. If it is cluttered, tidy it. If you cannot tidy the room easily, throw some things away. Your work with the Miracle Tree is more valuable than any ornament, toy, or possession. For obvious reasons, make sure that you will not be interrupted in any way. Turn off all electrical equipment, and, if possible, turn off "essentials" that usually run all the time in the background. Turning them off and back on again after you have practiced the form becomes part of the working. And who knows? Maybe you will discover that you do not need so many devices after all.

2. When you first begin to sense and feel the room, you may want to move some things. Often you will discover the room in a new way, and know that some items need to be moved or taken out altogether. Go with this new sense of place, and allow yourself time to make these changes.

   Do not concern yourself with techniques from books, such as arranging the room according to the principles of *fung shui* or changing the décor to include appropriate spiritual symbolism and colors. No matter how valuable these arts are in daily life, and in certain spiritual practices, what counts here is your own inner sense of the room, nothing else.

3. When you have participated in the form a few times, you will gradually discover the arrangement of the room that is right for you. Keep this arrangement for daily living in the room. Perhaps you have to move a few things for your work with the form each time you do it. Make this a ritual preparation, an integral part of your working.

4. Traditionally, the Qabalist often had a dedicated space, a room used only as a Temple. In this form, we are bringing the Temple into the ordinary room, so that room/temple-body/spirit will begin to interact continuously. Rather than leave the human world behind and enter the Temple, we bring the spirit into the human room by Breathing.

5. By working steadily with this form in any room, certain changes occur. The most significant changes will be in yourself, and you

will find that you can breathe any room effectively, once you have trained in the art. So any physical room with suitable proportions, anywhere, can become a cube of space, a vehicle for spiritual transformation. You do not become dependant on one location, but discover how to work in many with equal prowess.

6. If you work frequently in one room, the room will change. You will find that the spiritual forces strengthen and flow rapidly, and that your inner contact with angelic beings opens out substantially. In the living Qabalistic traditions, angels recognize the shape that you create when you breathe a room. They will respond to it. To you it is the cube of space, of the directions of the Planet, and of the universe. To the angels it is a Signature of Being, and a gateway of power. With time and practice, that is what it will become for you also.

7. Here is the curious part. Once you have attuned a room by using this form, you can also take it with you. Whenever and wherever you breathe a room, it is the same room, the same cube of space, time, and energy. So the inner room, the vehicle, becomes the reality within which you participate. Yet, we cannot do this so easily without first working with a physical outer room. In daily practice, projecting the breath onto the physical walls, ceiling, and floor (of any room anywhere) is what brings the inner vehicle to Life.

8. The first room that you work in is your training space, just like a gym, a dance studio, or a music room. Thereafter, you can take your

skills and development with you to any suitable space, and also transform that space, that room, by your skills.

9. Eventually the cube is hewn out of the space and time around you, and so it attunes your energy and consciousness. Once you are practiced in the form, you can create and enliven the cube anywhere.

There are many developments of this form, and it comprises an entire tradition of Qabalah within itself. Indeed, this Qabalistic method can be practiced without the Tree (and this may be its original form) or with the Tree growing on any or all of the four faces in the four directions, or in the center of the cube. In this form, the human body and the Tree of Life are one.

The Qabalah of Three Suns

This form is based on the reality of our relationship to the solar entities. Where is the nearest Sun? It is, of course, just beneath our feet, within the blazing heart of the Planet. The nearest Sun, the nearest Star, is very close to us...we live over it and around it, and we are always within its powerful energetic field. To the modern physicist it is the field of electro-magnetism, gravity, and myriad other measurable forces. To the old alchemists and magicians it was not the astral (starry) Light, but the Light of the Planet, the Earth Light. To the Qabalist, this radiance is a field of both energy and consciousness. Thus we have one Sun beneath us in the heart of the Earth, and another, as it seems, in the sky above us.

In truth the Sun that is *above* is often, relativistically, below or at an angle, or horizontal on one horizon or another due to the movement of our Planet around our central Star, our Sun, the heart of the Solar System. We will return to this relationship between the Sun and the horizons of East and West again, for it is central to much of practical Qabalah. Many of the so-called Secret Teachings are about how to relate to the Sun according to the Earth's rotation and orbit, through the subtle forces of the human body. Or to put it in another manner, about practical methods that lead to liberation from the dualism of "Light above" spirituality and dogma. Remember, the OverWorld Sun (in the sky) is frequently beneath us. So where is the real "above" and where the real "below"?

As humans living on the surface of the Planet, we are between two Suns, that which is above, and that which is below. Indeed, our very Being is enabled by the energies of these two Suns. The one above, our Star, gives the rhythm of light and dark, day and night and seasons, according to our planetary movement; the one below, burning within the planetary core of Earth, gives shape, form, and energy to the Planetary Being, of which we are part. Both Suns emit an immense spectrum of energetic forces, many of which are known to modern science, while others are known in the field of esoteric studies and metaphysics. The UnderWorld traditions, especially those of the faery races, titans, and giants, and UnderWorld deities, are all closely concerned with the planetary energies of the Earth Light...the *Sun at midnight* as it was called in the ancient Mysteries. When we find ways to participate in the interaction of energies and life-giving forces between the two Suns, we bring ourselves more truly alive. When you work with the Tree of Life, you will rapidly emerge from the old conditioned dualism, the propagandized ideas of above and below, higher and lower, heaven and hell. They simply do not exist in the way we have been led to believe by orthodox religions.

Above is actually Off Planet, while below is Within Planet. Providing we work with a *rooted* Tree of Life in our meditations and forms, we will free up from dualism. An unrooted Tree of Life, which emphasizes only the OverWorld, is a source of imbalance and spiritual enervation. Thus our work as Qabalists in the 21st century is to strengthen our relationship with the roots of the Miracle Tree, and to liberate the tradition from unhealthy dualism.

The following form is one that was originally a closely guarded "secret" technique, at the heart of many ancient magical traditions. This is precisely why the spiritual forces of the Earth Light and UnderWorld were so persistently vilified…they bring enlightenment and liberation.

The Qabalah of Three Suns involves the Sun Above, the Sun Below, and a third solar force, that which is our Heart of Being, in our own spiritual center. This is the Inner Sun. For practical purposes, we think of this deep in the center of the body, though it is in truth a spiritual or metaphysical direction or *locus* and not limited to a physical location.

Contrary to much modern dogma, it is not a *chakra* or an energy center, but is the *core* of Being, the source that generates such energy centers. Thus we might think of it as deeper in, and thus beyond the energy wheels or chakras, being, in truth, their source. There is a close analogy between the human energy centers or wheels (so flippantly popular in New Age spirituality) and weather patterns, tectonic movements on Earth, and solar flares and sunspots in the Sun, for they are all the energy wheels or spirals of power of the entities, greater or lesser, and each is generated and fed by a deeper source.

The simplest way to think of the Inner Sun is thus: it inhabits the central zone of the body. Thus it is traditionally related to the heart, yet it is not the physical organ that pumps blood. But paradoxically, we can come into communion with the Inner Sun by letting our awareness dwell upon the physical heart, and sensing its connection to the upper and lower entities, the two Suns on the OverWorld and UnderWorld. As with most of the direct forms, the secret of working with the Qabalah of Three Suns is in the inherent and ever-present connection between the entities, in this case the Sun above and the Sun below, and our physical body. Thus we work with Above, as in the above the head (Off Planet), Below as in beneath the feet (at the center of the Earth), and Within, the Sun and flame of our Being within. This form can be done with eyes open or eyes closed. It is a standing form, though it can also be done sitting (if you must).

The Three Suns

Part 1

1. Be still, enter Silence. Use the Stillness form.
2. Be aware of the physical Sun in the sky, the Sun Above. Let your awareness rest upon this entity...the physical Sun. Do not think of solar symbols, deities, colors, and attributes. Your awareness should rest upon the physical Sun, nothing more nor less.
3. Form a connection between your body and the physical Sun. Gradually the awareness of the physical Sun becomes an awareness of the solar illumination above you, linked to your body.
4. Let this awareness flow down through your body, into the Earth. Deep beneath your feet, discover the Sun Below. Let your awareness rest upon this physical entity, deep in the heart of the Planet.

5. Form a connection between your body and the physical Sun Below. Gradually your awareness comes into the underworld illumination below you, linked to your body.

6. Be still between the Sun Above and the Sun below. The entity above flows down through you, while the entity below flows upwards through you. Be still in the center; be aware of both entities and your connection to them.

7. Hold the awareness for at least five minutes. Return to your outer awareness by focusing on the natural sky above, and the land below. Let your sense of these steadily replace the illumination of the Suns Above and Below.

So ends the first part of the Qabalah of Three Suns. Practice this repeatedly before you move on to the subsequent parts of this form. Like most of the forms in this book, it is surprisingly easy to do once you translate it from the printed page into actual practice. Of course it is, because it works with a pattern that is already flowing through us. Our entire existence is lived out between the Sun above and the Sun below. The form opens us out to this aspect of our lives more fully, and reveals to us, as with all Tree of Life practices, that which is already there.

Part 2

Do not work with part 2 until you have practiced part 1. Only when you have a clear sense of the energies of the two Suns, above and below, should you move into this second phase.

1. Repeat stages 1-6 of part 1.

7. Let your awareness rest upon your heart, the spiritual heart at the mysterious center of your Being, physically in the hidden center of your

body. NOTE: do not equate this with any chakra practices that you know: if you do so, you will take the power out of the form and it will not work fully for you. You should think of the Inner Sun as being deeper than chakras, for it is the very heart and source of your Being.

8. Sense and feel the Sun Within come into radiance. It responds to the Sun Above and the Sun Below. Sense and feel the flow of illumination from below to above through your heart, and from above to below through your heart. Breathe steadily, and hold to the flow of the Suns. The third Sun, Within, will expand with the Inner Fire. NOTE: this stage can become ecstatic. Work with the Stillness Form if the heart forces become ecstatic, and hold them in balance.

9. Be Still, perfectly balanced around the Sun Within. You are the Three Suns.

10. Open your arms, holding them upwards and before you. Allow the power of the Three Suns to flow out before you. Next turn to your right, and repeat the opening. Likewise behind you, and then to your left. Return to facing the Direction in which you commenced. Close by sensing the four directions of the land, sensing, seeing, and feeling, that which is actually there in the environment around you. Sky above, land below. Conclude with the Crossing form if you wish.

So ends the second part of the Qabalah of Three Suns. Practice this frequently before you move on the third part.

Part 3

1. Repeat part 2, 1-10, but do not close.
2. Be aware again of the physical Sun Above, the physical Sun Below, and of their subtle illumination that flows through you.
3. Gradually sense that the Sun above descends to the western horizon behind you, while the Sun below simultaneously rises to the eastern horizon before you. They pivot around the Sun within, the inner Sun in the mysterious center of your Being. Now you have two Suns on the horizons.
4. Be Still, sensing, participating, and feeling the flow of power from the horizons.
5. Gradually sense that the Sun Before you (the Sun Below) rises to Above. As it does so, the Sun Behind you (the Sun Above) simultaneously descends to Below.
    Now you have the Sun above located Below, and the Sun below located Above.
6. Be still in this reversed solar pattern. Sense the forces flowing through the Sun Within.
7. Gradually sense that the UnderWorld Sun (Above) descends into your heart. As it does so the OverWorld Sun (Below) rises into your heart. They coalesce as One Sun, the Star Within. Be still in this coalescence.
8. Now the Sun Above rises out of your heart, to above your head. The Sun below descends to below your feet. You become aware again of the entities: the physical Sun above, the physical Sun below.

9. Let your awareness rest upon your heart, the Sun Within. Let its radiant forces flow through your entire body. Be Still as this triple solar power flows within you.

10. Close by being aware of sky above, land below, and the four directions of the Land. Use the Crossing form if you wish.

So we come to the end of the Qabalah of Three Suns.

Chapter 5

Imagination and the Tree of Life

One of the typical questions that people ask about Qabalah, the Tree of Life, and, indeed, all forms of meditation, visualization, and work with consciousness is, "is it all in my imagination?"

The answer is yes, just as the entire universe is "in the imagination." It might be more accurate to say that we are within the Imagination of the universe, but that the universe is not a product of our imaginings, and certainly not of our fantasies. Unfortunately our culture does little to distinguish between imagination and fantasy. This failure to discriminate between two very different zones or modes of consciousness has done us much harm. The thinly disguised prejudice against imagination in modernist culture is the direct heir of what used to be called the Christian work ethic…the idea that anything imaginative was idle, and had to be disposed of in favor of practical applications of thought. The exception to this disapproval was, and is, "valid" use of the mind, in science, logistics, and other "beneficial" modes. But no imagination, thank you.

Another disservice has been done to us by those affirmative therapies and meditations that, utterly misunderstanding Buddhism, say "all is mind," and that we "create our own reality." Too often this becomes a narcissistic meditation, in which the individual is deluded into contemplating a world that is the product of their egocentric obsessions…a world that does not exist. Such a concept is far indeed from the spiritual truth that All is Mind. The mind referred to is not that of the individual human personality, but of the universe. The Qabalist understands that All is Imagined, not by the ego-obsessed human, but by the Being that is the source of all Being.

To effectively alter "reality" through meditation, we must first discover our relative place and role in any consensual world. The Tree of Life offers substantial insights into this. As humans on Earth, we are primarily in the imagination of the Planet, and secondarily in the consciousness and energy of the land or zone in which we live. These potent fields of consciousness and energy interact with us, and, to use old-fashioned terminology, they dream us. It is for this very reason that all our work with the Tree of Life is empowered by our relationship to the directions, the land, the Under World of the Planet.

The inverse, yet direct relative of the widespread suspicion of the imagination (originally fostered by Christianity and upheld to this day in orthodox religions) is the progressive devaluation, manipulation, and trivializing of imagination in entertainment, greatly enhanced by our remarkable new technologies. The popular imagination becomes the fodder, and thereafter is regurgitated as the product of the entertainment industry. This mode or zone of consciousness is, strictly speaking, the realm of fantasy. But we have somehow forgotten that fantasy and imagination are not identical. One has to imagine to fantasize, or to enter into the products of fantasy in entertainment. But the imagination is capable of much more than entertaining fantasy. Fantasy is the crudest mode of the imagination, and has the potential to elevate or to debase us. If it is connected to deeper imaginative sources, to a tradition, to ethics, and in the case of the Qabalist, to the Tree of Life, fantasy becomes a useful servant. If it is disconnected and allowed to rule, fantasy can become a dangerous master.

The increased distribution of infantile fantasy in entertainment, seeming to be at its most trivial, yet most dangerous in violent computer games, serves only to separate us from both the results and the responsibilities of our actions. Violence is seen as a game, and winning is all. To the Qabalist, this is an unhealthy overemphasis of the forces of the 7th Emanation, Victory or Exaltation, while these forces are disconnected from the ethical and spiritual forces of the 8th and 6th Emanations.

What is the Imagination?

From a Qabalistic perspective, the imagination is the universe. All that is, is imagined by the divine source of Being. This is shown on the Tree of Life as the supernal Emanations, Crown, Wisdom, and Understanding. The impulse of Being to expand (2nd Emanation, Wisdom) is seeded into the containing vessel, its polar partner, in the universal depths (3rd Emanation, Understanding). Within the universal ocean of Being, primal forms or archetypes crystallize. *These are not the psychic archetypes as understood by modern psychology, but cosmic archetypes.* In the Platonic traditions within the foundations of Qabalah, such archetypes arise out of the interaction of time, space, and movement: they are universal Shapes. This is why, in our daily practices, many of the forms involve shape: the cube, the vertical, the sphere, the four or seven directions, and so forth. This method of working, a spiritual or sacro-magical *relativity*, relates directly to the energies of the land and Planet (as described previously in the context of who-imagines-what), but also extends to the Solar and Stellar Worlds.

The universal imagination arises as an impulse to expand, out of the Void, out of Stillness. This impulse generates movement, and that which moves is contained by a balancing power of contraction. These are shown on the Tree as the 2nd and 3rd Emanations, and also embodied by the Rod and Cup as conceptual implements for meditation, magic, and theurgy. The traditional implements are Sword, Rod, Cup, Shield, and Cord, which utilize the forces of Life, Light, Love, Law, and Truth, resonating through the elements of Air, Fire, Water, Earth, and their connection in Universal Spirit. Do not mistake these for symbols…they do not "represent" or "symbolize," as we so often say or read in many contexts. The implements of sacred magic, Sword, Rod, Cup, Shield, and Cord, have an inherent power and function because of their Shape. When you are practiced in the forms in this book, build some meditations upon the functions of the magical implements that are inherent in each form. Discover how they work for you, in you, around you, ceaselessly.

When the universal impulse to expand is restrained by the contracting or holding forces, shapes are generated. These are the relationships of the Emanations shown on the Tree of Life: the sphere, cube, pyramid or triangle, and many more. Such true archetypes (please remember, these are not the archetypes of psychology) are the first products of the Imagination of Being.

The progressive Emanation of the Tree of Life towards manifestation is a series of unfolding interacting images or shapes that arise from the process just described. This process has long been taught in Qabalistic tradition, and, morc rccently, modeled afresh by the discoveries of modern physics. Not so much discoveries, of course, as alternative statements or models of the universe. Long before Einstein, Qabalists understood the universe to be the manifest result of the interactions of Time, Space, and Energy. In metaphysics the term Movement often replaced that of Energy. We can also use the word Events—Time, Space, Events. There is no movement, no event, without energy.

From the archetypes or first shapes of the Imagination arise an infinite variety of others. Through many patterns of movement and containment, interacting within one another ceaselessly, we eventually come into manifestation in the Kingdom. Thus, in the Qabalistic traditions of the Tree of Life, Being imagines us...and so we come into Being. Another statement, and fascinating demonstration of this process is found in computer graphics, in the self-iterating fractal patterns such as the famous Mandelbrot set. These arise directly out of the interaction of numbers, just as the Tree of Life itself does. Thus technology shows that which has always been perceived in meditation and contemplation. Fractal images are a contemporary presentation of the dance of the elements or dance of number iterations in the universe. However, we must remind ourselves that these dancing self-iterating images are not imaginative in themselves: they are sterile or neutral patterns arising from inherent properties of number. They are not alive, nor do they have consciousness: they are simple statements, visual demonstrations of number patterns, rather than creators of pattern. Their significance lies in their demonstration of mathematical *shapes* at the very heart of numbers, of universal iterations. Fractals give interesting support to the ancient theory of the interaction of the elements, but they do not comprise the elements themselves so much as maps of elemental patterns within number relationships.

What of the human imagination?

We have within us a seed of the universal impulse to imagine…generating seed images or shapes-of-Being, such as those that appeared out of the interaction of the supernal Emanations previously. How could it be otherwise? We are part of that Imagination, we live within It, It lives within us. However, we do not often imagine at that primal level. The reasons proposed for our failure to realize our true powers of Imagination vary according to the tradition that you follow. In orthodox religion it is due to the fall from grace, to our seeking to usurp forbidden knowledge. Today we might see a new allegorical level of this ancient legend. Unethical use of technology (knowledge without Wisdom) separates us from our inner spirit, as we progressively exteriorize our imagination and refuse to take responsibility for our actions at a planetary level.

Imagination and the Abyss

In Qabalistic Understanding and tradition, our sense of alienation, and our divisive separation from spiritual comprehension is due to the creation phenomenon called the "Abyss," which is greatly misunderstood and misrepresented. The Abyss is simply the gap of space and time through which our energy moves. Or the difference between 0 and 1, 1 and 2, 2 and 3, out of which all other numbers arise. In the Stellar World, it is the vastness of interstellar time and space. In the human world it is, too often, the abyss of misunderstanding (3rd Emanation) between one human and another. In the individual it is the distance that we cross between our own states of consciousness: waking and sleeping, outer and inner, thinking and dreaming, life and death, death and rebirth.

The Abyss, like everything in the universe, has a three-fold nature. It is usually shown at the "top" of the linear Tree, as in our figure 1, by the Three Waves (look between the four dark lines) where it indicates the distance between our solar system and the Stars, and the difference between our type of consciousness within the Lunar and Solar Worlds, and the universal consciousness of the stellar or supernal Emanations. These are the first three spheres or Emanations that are described as "brooding over the Abyss." This terminology gives us a valuable insight, for it means brooding as in gestating or sitting on eggs (not the more modern meaning of moodiness, which is derived from the deeper idea of brooding).

The Threefold Abyss: least, lesser, greater.

The least and invisible abyss is between Earth and Moon, between our bodies and our thoughts, feelings, and vital forces. We cross and recross this constantly. Yet despite our deep familiarity with the journey, we feel alienated and it has become a feature of modern concern in self-development and therapy. The next or lesser abyss is the one between the Lunar World or Triad, and the Solar. This is the distance between the Foundation of Earth and Moon (10th and 9th Emanations) and the Sun and Planets. It is also the difference between our earthy or outwardly focused consciousness, and the spiritual or inwardly focused consciousness that discovers that it is part of a greater whole. The lesser abyss is crossed in meditation, in certain dreams, and at key moments in any lifetime. Sometimes it is crossed during orgasm, when the Lovers feel radiant ecstatic energies.

The Great Abyss, the one shown in a standard Tree of Life, has been described.

The universal Being moves through space and time, and by interactions generates shapes and patterns: in this way Being imagines Being. The imagination is defined as *the power to create images of potential manifestation.* Some of these images or archetypes do not come into manifestation. Some manifest swiftly. The same is true of the human imagination: anyone who has ever imagined anything will confirm this.

On the Tree of Life, the imagination of the human moves either outward towards manifestation…moving with one universal current, or inward towards its creative source, moving with the other universal current. As we are on the outer rim of creation, so to speak, it is the indrawing power of limitation and Severity, or the left hand pillar of the Tree, that is of most significance to us in Qabalistic practice. Until we have gained some skill in working with inwardly directed imagination, we cannot use the imagination creatively.

The Three modes of Imagination

The Tree of Life reveals three modes or depths of imagination, within the realms of Moon, Sun, and Stars. The human imagination, reaching within, discovers three levels or modes. In their universal context, they are the three stages of Emanation that resonate, interact, and create the Three Worlds of Stars, Sun, and Moon. In their human context, they are discovered as three states of consciousness that lead progressively to deeper imagination and eventually bring us to Wisdom and Understanding of truth.

The three modes or states of consciousness are defined in esoteric tradition by the Three Wheels of Fortune, Justice, and Judgment on the Tree of Life, represented by the tarot trumps of the same name. Most of our general fantasy, focused or unfocussed, orbits around the Path of Fortune, bouncing to and fro between thought and feeling (8th and 7th Emanations,

Scintillation/Mercury and Exaltation/Venus). It is generally fuelled or supported by our Life forces and sexuality (9th and 10th Emanations, Foundation, Moon), but also strengthened by collective and ancestral streams of consciousness (9th and 10th Emanations).

At this level of the imagination, we find most commercial entertainment. Such entertainment has replaced, almost entirely, the older ancestral tales and songs and ceremonies that were once part of human life. We have lost the ancestral traditions and replaced them with television and computers. In this process, greatly accelerated in the last 50 years, we have effectively begun to exteriorize our imagination. We will return to this idea shortly.

The popular entertainment of modernism varies considerably: some is of inspiring quality, while some is degenerate and unhealthy. Most is a mixture. As a rule, general entertainment does not reach beyond the wheel of Fortune. Indeed, the manipulative aspects of entertainment and advertising, news and propaganda, are intentionally designed to keep us within that wheel. But we also find that the great music, art, and literature of our world, are likewise in the zone of consciousness that we call the Wheel of Fortune, the Path between Mind and Feeling. However, such material leads us, through its images, concepts, and emotional impulses, towards the second level, shown by the Path and wheel of Justice. In some examples, such as those of religion, mysticism, and magical traditions, the words, images, patterns, and sounds, have an intentional quality: they are designed and presented in order for our imagination to be stimulated towards an altered consciousness, beyond the repetitions of the wheel of Fortune. In many other examples, not formally part of a spiritual tradition, the material embodies the altered consciousness, calls to us, and inspires us. It is spiritual because the Universal Spirit has spoken to the artist, rather than through spiritual involvement in a formal tradition or religion.

When we come into the second wheel, that of Justice, the Path between the 5th and 4th Emanations (Severity and Mercy, Mars and Jupiter), the imagination is fuelled not by the Moon, but by the Sun, the 6th Emanation. At this level, we find the cycle of creative and destructive forces shown in the spokes or branches, those Paths that radiate in the heart of the Tree of Life. The imagination reaches beyond self, beyond fantasy, daydream, gratification, and habit.

In our work with the Tree of Life, this, more than any other, is where we should seek to cleanse and purify our individual imaginings. When we do so, they increasingly partake of the forces of the Solar Triad. If we do not work on this cleansing (5th Emanation) we become imbalanced: the forces of the Emanations will be drawn back into the cycle of Fortune, sometimes powerfully enhanced, and can lead to obsession, addictive fantasies, and (occasionally) to physical action based on unhealthy fantasy. If we can imagine it, we can do it. Our imaginings should be cleansed and purified, so that when we act, we act with an ethical and compassionate focus.

Most of our work with forms, and many of the associated Qabalistic arts, are about purifying the imagination, and, at a later stage, shaping it. In practice, we tend to work on the cleansing and the shaping simultaneously. The forms, meditations, and visions both transform and shape our consciousness, which is to say, our imagination. The deeper you reach into your consciousness, the nearer you come to the spiritual imagination. The further you exteriorize your consciousness and lose awareness of its depths, the nearer you come to being trapped within a manifest form that is closed to spiritual imagination. Such barriers are broken down during crises, and at death. They are never permanent, but they seem to be especially dominant in our culture during this age of hi-tech tools and toys and rapid travel.

The third level of the Imagination is, to us, abstract. It is the Path and wheel of Judgment, between Wisdom and Understanding. It is found in the depths of consciousness, where primal Archetypes or Shapes arise. Please remember that these are *not* the archetypes popular in modern psychology, and you should not confuse the two terms and definitions in your meditations.

Many of the more abstract Qabalistic practices involve meditations on Shape: in the Neo-Platonic or Hermetic traditions, the Qabalist meditates *within* the Platonic Solids, not as cardboard cutouts or models made of wire, but in the living consciousness. These Solids are three-dimensional shapes, such the sphere, the Cube within the sphere, the Pyramids on the faces of the Cube, and so forth. The meditator *imagines* such Shapes about his or her self, and interacts with them in altered consciousness. Such imagination is very different from a self-gratifying fantasy, and requires skill, patience, focus, and discipline. The Shapes are also modeled or reflected in the outer world by the sacred geometry of our ancient sites, temples, churches, and power places.

We can also come into the third mode of Imagination through Stillness. With continued stillness meditations, such as the Stillness form, we allow the deeper imagination to flow through us. When we do so, it brings wordless Wisdom, and formless Understanding. It may also bring visions of archetypes, the shapes that arise during the primal interactions of Time, Space, and Energy.

The Imagination in Daily Practice

When we work with the Miracle Tree, the imagination is vital to us. The Qabalistic forms and practices will enhance and energize the imagination, and gradually move it deeper into Solar and Stellar realms, through the zones of Justice and Judgment. Many of the classic meditations and visions involve *telesms*, which are images of gods and goddesses, angels and archangels, places, people, and powers. Such images are generated by the forces of Fortune, and are always regarded as our practical means rather than ends in themselves. It is at this level that the spiritual psychology and the materialistic psychologies begin to share some concepts. The seemingly random or dream-like images that are called "archetypes" in popular psychology are the images of the wheel of Fortune. They are usually limited to the recycling process of the individual psyche, though some have a collective, tribal, and ancestral quality. Thus they can include deities, ancestors, family, and images of almost anything pregnant with meaning for the individual. But such images are disconnected from deeper forces until we work with them consciously, not in therapy, but in meditation, contemplation, and inner vision.

Certain *telesms* or divine images endure through the centuries, as many people have worked with them: others are the special properties of magical traditions, or specific inner temples and lines of initiation. Yet they all branch into one another in many ways, with many organic connections.

In all magical and spiritual traditions, such random but identifiable images that come in dreams, that constitute the silent alphabet of our processes of thoughts and feelings, a process beneath that of conscious interaction or the outer concept of self, are taken and transformed. No longer are they random images from conditioning, from experiences, from ancestral or even genetic continuity, but they become focused and attuned images that receive the spiritual forces of the next wheel, of the Solar Triad. Once we begin this process, we strengthen the forces of the Lunar Triad where such images are automatically generated, maintained, and stored. The word automatically does not imply machine-like, but refers to the constant organic generation of images in the 9th Emanation, images that come and go ceaselessly. Some are enduring and specific, others are ephemeral and they are loose or ambiguous. When we work with them consciously, we also transform and purify them within ourselves: by doing so, we transform our vital energies and direct them towards the deeper realms of the imagination. If we do not cleanse them, they can become sources of disruption and imbalance. This is closely connected to an idea discussed in our earlier chapter on angels and messengers, for in traditional Qabalah, it is taught that there are orders of spiritual beings in the Lunar World who travel to and fro between humanity and greater awareness. These are said, traditionally, to be "made wise" by the prayers and dreams of humanity.

In addition to using forms, meditations, visions, and ceremonies, we should also guard and cleanse our imagination in a day-to-day sense. This is especially important at the beginning of your Qabalistic work, and, paradoxically, when we reach an advanced stage in our spiritual transformation. There is a spiraling phenomenon that occurs in spiritual work: when we are "advanced," we face again the so-called problems or weaknesses that we thought we had left behind, though they manifest in new and often unexpected ways. This is because they are the pressure points of power that we chose when we were born, and they have to be resolved fully in any one lifetime before they cease to reoccur.

164 🎋 The Miracle Tree

Miracles and the Imagination

To gain real miracles, we must discover how and where our inner forces are weakened, drained, and subverted. In our current modernist culture, this is often through popular entertainment, and especially through media that involve visuals: television, film, and computers. They drain us because they *exteriorize* the imagination, placing images upon a screen, rather than in our inherent vision and image-making field of consciousness. Please note that I am not talking about content or quality, only about the exteriorization of the imagination through placing images outside the living consciousness. Part of the addiction of television and computer entertainment lies in this simple fact that the images are outside ourselves, and we are passive to them. This does not occur when the imagination is engaged inwardly, and we interact with images within our consciousness.

The Imagination is a Muscle

The serious practitioner of any spiritual art or discipline should cut down on television and computer entertainment. Such media tend toward an addictive exteriorization of the imagination...and like all muscles that are not used properly, the imagination will atrophy. Using media as the main, or (in most cases today) the only source of stimuli for the imagination, is comparable to using a mechanical and electronic exoskeleton to move your body. While this may be useful in some cases of extreme disability, it is artificially unnecessary for most of us. The imagination is the most powerful muscle we have. Do not trap it inside a plastic box and limit it to cartoon entertainment.

There are, of course, many other areas in which we can clarify our imagination. Fantasies about power, sex, revenge, love, hate, and self-aggrandizement are the classic follies of the imagination. Some rare individuals are driven to become monsters by such fantasies, and none of us are free from them. Nowadays media generally exteriorizes such fantasies, but the old-fashioned versions, those interior self-inflating fantasies, are still a potential problem for anyone seeking spiritual transformation.

In many traditional Paths to Wisdom, the self-inflating fantasies are regarded as "unclean" or "evil." Today we could rightly assert that they can lead to evil behavior if they are acted out in the human world, or that they can pollute the vital forces, clouding them and obscuring our deeper spiritual perceptions and imagination.

The Tree of Life shows us a number of ways of cleansing and refining the imagination, and of alchemically transforming the fantasies into images that embody the sacred. When we do so, the energy is taken out of the fantastical and self-aggrandizing realm into one of focused power.

Most of the basic methods are old-fashioned: discipline of mind and body, and most significant, ongoing disengagement from unhealthy imagery (both outward and inward) through all and any means possible. There is no point in throwing your television out of the window if you continue to fantasize along the lines of a cruel and sexually explicit drama, or if you succumb to daydreaming about the lifestyles and wealth of media stars. There is little value in erasing shoot-em-up, hack-em-down, and occult fantasy games from your hard drive if you still relive their basic urges and thrills in your down time as self-comforting delusions.

However, if you work with the god and goddess images, the telesms of the Tree of Life, they will take and transform such energies, tendering them to you again in a new manner. If you steadily practice the forms offered in this book, you will find that the relationship between your vital forces and your imagination changes substantially, and continues to change. The Tree of Life is a tree of changes, and its miracles are those changes that we least expect.

Chapter 6

Forms for Working with the Tree of Life

These short forms are intended to be one-page workings that you can easily learn, practice, and memorize. Work with them in order, one at a time, until you are familiar with them. Do not attempt to try them all without practice. Steady progress will repay your effort, so stay with each of these short forms, become practiced in it, then move on to the next.

After the 10 short forms is a classic Qabalistic form: The *External Vision of the Tree*. This form is most effective after you have developed your skills with the 10 short forms, and with the longer forms in the preceding chapters. Projecting the Tree of Life, as described in The External Vision, is one of the enduring Qabalistic arts, and has much potential hidden within it.

Short Form 1: Stilling Time, Space, and Movement

Sit with eyes closed, free of interruption. With practice you will be able to do this with eyes open, while moving.

1. TIME: withdraw your involvement in time…find yourself time-free, then timeless.

    SPACE: draw in your awareness from all directions, releasing your involvement with space. Rest on a simple point of Being within you.

    MOVEMENT: Cease all outer and inner movement, but for breathing in and out.

2. Reach within yourself to the Unbeing out of which your Being comes. The Stillness that precedes movement, the Silence between each Breath. This is the Void that is within all things, the source of all Time, Space, and Movement.

3. Let yourself Unbe.

4. Affirm the Four Directions, Above, Below, and Within. (Begin any meditation or ceremony now).

5. Chant: use the vowel sounds **O A I.** Chant each one on a long low tone. The O stills Time. The A draws in space to the center. The I is the flame of Being. At the end of the chant, the Flame draws into the Void, into Unbeing.

6. Phrase for inner Contemplation: "Peace is a Secret Unknown."

Short Form 2: The Crossing

This is an essential Qabalistic working, which has much deep potential within it. Use this on its own, and briefly before and after each meditation or working. This should be spoken aloud. May also be whispered. The right hand is usually used for the movements.

1. "In the Name of the Wisdom" (hand upwards to top of forehead).
2. "The Love" (hand downwards towards genitals).
3. "The Justice" (to right shoulder).
4. "The Infinite Mercy" (across to left shoulder).
5. "Of the One Eternal Spirit" (circle right and downwards from top of forehead, to genitals, completing left and upwards back to top of forehead).
6. "AMEN" (hummed resonantly).

The Circle is the sphere of Being. The centerline of your body is Stars/head, Sun/heart, and Moon/genitals to feet. Affirm the Four Directions and Powers around you. Be still.

Alternative crossing formula, using the same hand movements.

1. "In the Name of the Star Father."
2. "The Deep Mother."
3. "The True Taker."
4. "The Great Giver."
5. "We are one Being of Light."
6. AMEN.

You may expand the Crossing to a meditation on each of the points in turn: above the head, below the genitals, to your right, to your left, and the sphere of unity. Find communion with the spiritual powers described in the Crossing formulas.

Do this at least once a day.

Short Form 3: Earth, Moon, Sun, and Stars

May be done sitting, standing, or walking.

Begin by being Still, stilling Time, Space, and Movement.

1. Sit facing East. Affirm each Direction about you: East/South/West/North. Sky Above, Land Below. Being Within.

2. Direct attention to your feet. "My feet are of the Earth." Feel the *physical* Earth power flow through your feet.

3. Direct attention to your genitals. "My genitals are of the Moon." Feel the power rise into your genitals, and visualize the Lunar power descending from the *physical* Moon to merge with it.

4. Direct attention to your center, your heart. "My heart is of the Sun." Feel the combined Earth and Lunar power rise into your Heart, and visualize the Solar power descending from the *physical* Sun to merge with it.

5. Direct attention to your head. "My head is in the Stars." Feel the combined Earth, Lunar, and Solar forces rise into the Head. Visualize the Stellar power descending from the *physical* Stars to merge with it.

6. Be still, silent, and poised. Feel the perfect balance of these physical and spiritual forces within you, between Above and Below, at the Center of the Directions.

7. Affirm the Directions again, and make the Crossing Sign. Your meditation is complete.

Short Form 4: The 4 Archangels of the Directions

May be done sitting, standing, or walking.

Be still, stilling Time, Space, and Movement. If sitting or standing still, face East. If walking, use "Before you" as the East, no matter what direction you are walking in.

1.   In the East, or Before you, is the archangel Raphael, bearer of the Sword, bringer of Instruction and Inspiration. Mediator of the divine powers of Life, and of the element of Air. Sense, feel, and see the presence of this spiritual power. Breathe deeply in and out, and feel the Air in your breath and in your lungs fill with the power of Raphael.

2.   In the South, or to your Right, is the archangel Michael, bearer of the Spear, bringer of Initiation and Illumination. Mediator of the divine powers of Light, and of the element of Fire. Sense, feel, and see the presence of this spiritual power. Feel your blood and your inner Fire of vitality coursing through you, filled with the power of Michael.

3.   In the West, or Behind you, is the archangel Gabriel, bearer of the Vessel, bringer of Giving and Receiving. Mediator of the divine powers of Love and compassion, and of the element of Water. Sense, feel, and see the presence of this spiritual power. Feel the Water that makes up most of your body respond and become charged with the power of Gabriel.

4.   In the North, or to your Left, is the archangel Auriel, bearer of the Shield, bringer of Destruction and Regeneration. Mediator of the divine powers of Law and Wisdom, and the element of Earth. Sense, feel, and see the presence of this spiritual power. Feel the bones and minerals of your body respond and become charged with the strength of Auriel.

5.   Be Still, communing with all Four archangels, sensing the Stars above, and the Land beneath your feet. Make the Crossing Sign, and quietly honor and close the Contacts in each direction. Your meditation is complete.

Short Form 5: The Tree of Life and Your Body

This form begins with the 10th Emanation, progresses to the 1st Emanation, then back through the body in conclusion and completion, to the 10th Emanation. May be done sitting, standing, or walking.

Begin by being Still, stilling Time, Space, and Movement.

10. My feet walk steadily upon the Earth that supports me.
9. My genitals receive and give forth the sacred power of the Moon.
8. My right hip is a center of Scintillating power.
7. My left hip is a center of Victorious peace.
6. My heart is radiant with Beauty.
5. My right hand is Just and Truthful.
4. My left hand is Merciful and Compassionate.
3. About my right shoulder and head is Understanding.
2. About my left shoulder and head is Wisdom.
1. Above my head is the Crown of Being.
10. My entire body is the realm of the King and Queen of Peace.
9. My dreams and visions are Pure and clear as Moonlight.
8. My mind composes thoughts with Honor and integrity.
7. My feelings and senses are dedicated to divine awareness.
6. The center of my Being is Harmonious, and Knows Truth.
5. My sense of discipline and Severity is impersonal and calm.
4. My sense of creating and giving is beyond thought of return or benefit.
3. The great ocean of Understanding flows into my contemplation.
2. The Wisdom of the Stars reflects within me.
1. My breath is the Breath of the Spirit of Life breathing through me.

Make the Crossing Sign. Your meditation is complete.

Short Form 6: Gods and Goddesses

This form begins with the 10th Emanation of Earth, and progresses sequentially to the 1st Emanation. Note: you may use deities from other pantheons if you prefer, providing they have the 10 functions and powers described. May be done sitting, standing, or walking.

Begin by being Still, stilling Time, Space, and Movement.

10. In the Kingdom of Earth, the Earth Mother, Strong and not lightly moved.

9. In the Foundation of the Moon, the White Queen and her Dark Sister.

8. In the Glory of Mercury, the swift hermaphrodite god of Brilliance.

7. In the Victory of Venus, the goddess of triumphant exalted senses and shared Love.

6. In the Beauty of the Sun: the Bright One that partakes of All yet is bound by None.

5. In the Severity of Mars: the strict goddess of destruction and purification.

4. In the Mercy of Jupiter: the god of creation and expansion.

Through the depths of Pluto, the Bridge Maker, across the Abyss between the Worlds:

3. In the Understanding of Saturn, the Great Mother of Time, Space, and Stillness.

2. In the Wisdom of Neptune, the Star Father of the Universe and Movement.

1. In the mystery of Uranus, at the Threshold of the Void, the One Being that utters All Being.

Short Form 7: The Vision of the Hall of Light

1. Work with this first as a story that you read, then as a guided vision that you build by reading the text aloud to yourself. When you are familiar with the vision, work without the text. Refer back to it from time to time if you need, but gradually build this essential Qabalistic vision in your full awareness, and enter the Hall of Light in Silence.

2. At the outset of this practice, work while sitting still with eyes closed; this is the usual method for entering the Inner Halls of the Tree of Life. Later you may work with eyes open, and even while walking. Entering the Hall may be integrated with a specific route that you walk, including or concluding with a seated meditation.

3. Keep a short handwritten record of your experiences. The handwriting is important in this work, for the digits of the fingers reproduce the Emanations and Paths of the Tree of Life in miniature. The pen that you hold is a Rod or Staff, directing the sacred letters that flow. Within, the pen is a Vessel or Cup, holding the ink, while at its scribing point it is a Blade or Sword. The surface of the pen, held in your hand, is a Shield or Manifest Shape, as is the paper on which you inscribe your book of Wisdom. Make the handwriting a ritual: you may be surprised at the ideas that come to you when you write your meditational journal in this conscious manner.

Begin by being Still, stilling Time, Space, and Movement.

1. With your inner senses, see and feel before you a door of Fire, guarded by two mighty beings, each with many wings and many eyes, each bearing a flaming sword held up to create the arch of the door. Be still, and form your calm intent to enter the Hall of Light, where the Mysteries of the Tree of Life are received, taught, and practiced.

2. The door opens, and you pass within, to climb a long staircase of Stars. You feel invisible, beings uplift and strengthen you on right and left.

3. Before you as you climb is a high radiant arch, and as you approach, you find that it reaches to the heights and is founded in the depths of the universe. As you draw close, it changes size to human proportions, and you pass within.

4. The Hall of Light has many pillars; each of changing colors, and in the center is the Living Flame of Being. Commune here in silence and stillness.

5. Now others become apparent to you: angels, spiritual beings, and mentors, fellow visionaries that will work with you.

6. Exchange, learn, and commune. Here also share devotion at the Source of the Living Flame. Here a vision of the Perfect Tree may be discovered.

7. Return from the Hall of Light, down the Stair of Stars, out the Door of Fire, to the human world. Bring the power of that place with you as a gift to the world.

Short Form 8: The Cube of Presence

This meditation strengthens and defines your awareness of the spiritual forces. It also builds and creates an interface for communion and exchange of energies with angelic and other spiritual beings. In essence it is very simple, and like the Tree of Life, of which it is a part, it works with that which is Already Present within all things. Initially, work with part 1 only until you are familiar with it. Next add part 2. Finally add part 3, until you are able to work with all three parts.

Part One

1. The Crossing.
2. The Stillness.
3. Affirm the 7 Directions.
4. Build your awareness of the sphere of Being about you.
5. Before you, build the Eastern face of the Cube within the sphere. Shape it out of radiance, with thin lines of Light defining it. Let the inside of the face be Clear. Repeat this for the South, West, and North faces. Then the face Above, and the face Below.
6. You have built a clear cube, defined by radiant lines of Light that fits perfectly within the sphere of Being. Be still, and hold your sense of the cube.
7. Commune in silence. (*If you stop at this point*, when you are ready, let the cube fade to each direction. Make the crossing, and return to your outer awareness.)

Part Two

Affirm the presence of the Elements and Four archangels directly within the faces of the cube. Affirm the Divine Presence above, the Earth below, and being in the center, within you. Let the faces of the cube act as exchange zones for the spiritual forces.

Part Three

Work with the faces of the cube to mediate and give out the spiritual forces to the outer world, in all directions. Keep handwritten notes of how this develops and what may arise spontaneously within the working.

Short Form 9: Externalizing the Crossing

This working is done from within that altered state of consciousness created by any of the others. It should not be done from an outer state, and not be undertaken superficially or as a mere formula.

1. Raise the right arm towards a direction (before you) and extend Upwards. Sense the power flowing through you and out of the extended arms and hand. It flows to the threshold that you set…the limits of the circle, sphere, room, location, and so forth.

2. Recite the Crossing, making the hand movements towards the direction/location, but not over yourself, as you have already done the Crossing for yourself before this externalizing.

3. The first movement is *Up/Wisdom, Down/Love*. This is a straight line from Above to Below, in the center of the direction.

4. The second movement is *Right/Justice, Left/Mercy*. This is made from far right to far left, midway across the centerline. You reach the right extreme by curving your arm movement up from Below, out to the right. Then straight across to the left.

5. The third movement is *Completion/Spirit*. This curves from the left upwards to Above, and then continues around the entire circle, until you come back to Above.

6. Repeat this for all Four Directions, turning to face each one.

7. Sense, feel, and see, that the Above and Below of each crossing extend and come together. Likewise the Right and Left of each crossing. Thus you came back to a sphere, but externally resonating in the defined working space. Commune and meditate within this resonant space.

Note 1: You may do this with one direction only for a shorter training session or any working that focuses on what is in that direction.

Note 2: You may externalize the crossing to charge, or bless, or protect an object, a person, a place, and so forth. But always work from within an altered state arising from other Tree of Life workings; never do this as a mere formula.

Short Form 10: Breathing

Begin by being Still, stilling Time, Space, and Movement.
Use the Crossing formula.

1. Breathe in and out simply, reaching into Stillness within you. Use long deep breathes, and when you have practiced this, you may build to a brief pause between in and outgoing breath.

2. The in-breath contains the hidden sound AH. Form this in your imagination as you breath in, hear it in the sound of your breath in your skull.

3. The out-breath contains the hidden sound IH. Form this in your imagination as you breath in, hear it in the sound of your breath in your skull.

4. Being still, utter the hidden sound AHIH, the first Breath of Being.

5. Discover that your in-breath is the out-breath of Being. Discover that your out-breath is the in-breath of Being. Thus Being breathes you.

6. When Being breathes you, let the utterance of AH become "I" and the utterance of IH become "AM." Discover that you are breathed, with your physical breath, by the universal I AM.

7. Utter the chant of I A O to still Time, Space, and Movement. Be still, and let the breath settle in silence.

Your Breathing I AM is complete.

The External Vision of the Tree of Life

Begin by being Still, stilling Time, Space, and Movement.

This may be undertaken with eyes open or closed. This form is at its most powerful when you work with eyes open, for the eyes project the Tree of Life to the space before you. You could use a wall as the Mirror or Shield for this form, or you may choose to build the Tree in the space before you.

Build in your inner vision, appearing before you, the Middle Pillar of the Tree of Life: four spheres linked by vertical Paths.

1. Begin at the Crown above (sphere 1), with a sphere of clear illumination, the Star.
2. Continue to Beauty, in the center (sphere 6), with a sphere of radiant yellow gold, the Sun.
3. Continue to Foundation (sphere 9), with a sphere of deep violet radiating silver, the Moon.
4. Conclude at the Kingdom (sphere 10), with a sphere of earthen brown and green, the world of Earth.

Build in your inner vision, appearing before you, the Three Crossings or Wheels.

5. Below the Crown, the Crossing of Judgment, linking Wisdom (sphere 2) and Understanding (sphere 3). See and feel Wisdom as a sphere of silver gray on the right, and Understanding as a sphere of impenetrable black on the left. See them linked by a horizontal Path. Complete the triangle between them by linking the Crown both to Wisdom and to Understanding.

6. Above Beauty, the Crossing of Justice, linking
    Mercy (sphere 4) and Severity (sphere 5), see
    and feel Mercy as a sphere of sky blue on the
    right, and Severity as a sphere of blood red on
    the left. See them linked by a horizontal Path.
    Complete the triangle between them by link-
    ing Beauty to both Mercy and Severity.

7. Above Foundation, see the Crossing of For-
    tune, linking Victory (sphere 7) and Glory
    (sphere 8). See and feel Victory as a sphere
    of verdant green on the right, and Glory as a
    sphere of vibrant orange on the left. See them
    linked by a horizontal Path. Complete the tri-
    angle by linking Foundation to both Victory
    and Glory.

As you hold this vision before you, the radiant Paths
all appear and complete the Tree of Life. Hold it in your
inner vision and feel your body and your awareness respond to it. When you are ready, conclude your vision
with Silence and Stillness once more.

Chapter 7

The Paths of the Tree of Life

In the last part of Chapter 3, we developed the Bridge Building form. This is adapted from the ancient technique of what is nowadays loosely called "Path working." Originally, Path working was a form of visionary meditation, sometimes allied with ritual that sought to work with any Path of the Tree of Life. A Path is the fusion of two Emanations or spheres, bringing their spiritual forces into balance, through us. Nowadays "Path working" is used very loosely to mean almost any guided visualization, regardless of its content. In this book, Path working always holds to its original meaning, an experience of two Emanations, ideally simultaneously, resonating through the human being.

Anyone who meditates upon the Miracle Tree for any length of time will rapidly realize that the Paths are more significant for us than the single Emanations or individual spheres. The Paths are significant in the sense of interaction, of spiritual transformation, and of changes of

Understanding within us. Human growth and change works through interaction. But there is more.

When you build the Bridge, and stand upon its threshold, angelic beings come to your right and left to strengthen and uphold you. They always come, at death, at birth, in meditation. They come because that is their universal function and power, not because they have any personal interest in us. Indeed, they are not aware of us as personalities or as humanocentric individuals, much as we might wish them to be.

Do you notice any similarity between this tradition of bridge-building, angelic support, and the concept of Path working? Good. Then you already know what Path working entails, and with your bridge building you have already laid a foundation for your Path working.

In the simplest, yet most powerful, Qabalistic arts, the Qabalist calls upon the angels or archangels of two Emanations, one to the right, one to the left, at the threshold of the Bridge. The angelic forces literally hurl the Qabalist over the bridge, projected, as he or she must be, between the polarized powers of the two Emanations. This is Path working. Are you ready for it?

The Paths of the Tree of Life

There are 22 Paths on a classic Tree of Life. Each Path is a fusion or totality of two Emanations. This is shown clearly in figure 1. When the spiritual forces of two Emanations combine, that is a Path.

This approach to Path Working is somewhat different than the idea that the Paths "connect" the Emanations or spheres. The Emanations are within one another, as in figure 2, and are not separate or isolated from one another. Once again, the linear nature of images on paper creates a false impression: that of the Tree of Life as a board game, with stations connected by Paths. Or the Tree is a circuit diagram, with components connected by circuitry. None of this is inaccurate, and there are many insights to be found by following such ideas in meditation. Yet they create a sense of linear progression, of essential division that is not inherent in the Tree itself. In other words, they are helpful analogies at the outset of Qabalistic work, but they soon evaporate if you participate in the Tree at a deeper lever of understanding.

The three modes of the Paths

There are three modes or aspects of each Path. Two are directional or circulatory, and one is dynamic or total. Let us examine this idea in more detail. It derives from the simple truth of how a tree lives. Our trees in the forests draw from below, through their roots, and transmit to above, through the trunk, branches, and leaves. Likewise, they receive from above, and transmit to below. This circulatory flow is what sustains our atmosphere, and all life on Earth depends upon it.

The organic tree embodies the cosmic Tree. The Tree of Life has its roots in the UnderWorld, the realm of the planetary core, and its Crown in the Stars. It transmits from the Sun within the Earth, to the Sun in the sky, to the Stars. Likewise, it simultaneously receives and sends spiritual forces from the Stars, to the Sun, to the depths of the Earth. This cosmic aspect of the Tree is shown also by the radiant energies (light, radiation, electro-magnetism, and so forth) that are emitted by the Planet, Sun, and Stars, which exchange and interact with one another. Thus the Paths have a natural directional and circulatory nature. For us as humans, this depends on how we relate to each Path, for each exchanges equally between its two Emanations. We could move in either direction, toward either Emanation/sphere.

This directional movement is what we might think of as the natural flow of the Tree. But Qabalistic Path working consists of being infused with the forces of two Emanations at once, a totality rather than a movement toward or away from one or the other.

In associative and exploratory meditations, we can use the Paths to move from one sphere to the other, to climb the Emanations to the Stars, to circulate the Great Wheel of life, death, and rebirth, stage by stage. In Path working, something different happens: the archangels and angels and forces of pairs of Emanations move us into altered states of consciousness and energy. In traditional Qabalah, these are often called Halls, and are described as spirit-places or locations.

So when you think of the Paths, come away from the board game or circuitry analogy toward experience of totalities. Each Path is a totality, a unity of two potent Emanations. How was this kind of experience taught, handed down, and experienced?

In oral tradition, at a time when little was written down, the record of spiritual experience was preserved in inspired chant, poetry, or narratives. Such verses or accounts form the basis for the entire Qabalistic tradition formalized in the Middle Ages with commentaries. All traditional mythology, fairy lore, and esoteric legend worldwide contains narrative journeys. Some of them, such as those from the myths of ancient cultures, are well known to us. Many are not. Sometimes such stories, as the essentially Qabalistic tale of Er in Plato's *Republic* (*see Appendix B*), give detailed instructions on what happens in spiritual dimensions. In others, the material is less coherent, less formalized.

Such accounts are not, however, a "journey" or guided visualization in the contemporary New Age or therapeutic sense. The images and the journey arise out of the spiritual flight...they are reports, and not contrivances assembled to create a mood, sustain energy, or bring tranquility. This is true also of the traditional descriptions of deities: the descriptions arise from experiencing the power...they are not checklists of symbols assembled around an anthropomorphic image. This difference may seem petty to our modern minds, but it is vital to working magic and mysticism with the Tree of Life.

There are, in fact, *no words* for any Path working. The words are only your report of what you experienced. But as we know, it is traditional to take the reports of those spiritual scouts, explorers, and mentors, who have gone before, and use these as indicators of what we might expect when we follow them. This is the basis of the oral Qabalah that underpins, or should underpin, any written text.

Path Triads and Tarot Trumps

The Paths on the Tree of Life arise out of the interaction of the Emanations. They are always in sets of three, with primary Path Triads, and secondary Path Triads. In each of the Path Triads, be they primary or secondary, there are also complimenting pairs of Paths, which tend to reflect the polarities of the Emanations that they connect. This same threefold pattern runs through everything that we are: Positive/Negative/Balanced. When we find it in Three Triads of Emanation (Lunar, Solar, Stellar) we also find three sets of Paths linking each Triad. These are the Path Triads. You can see these easily as the triangles made on the Tree by the connections between the Emanations or spheres. Figure 1 shows the basic Tree of Life, while figure 12 shows tarot trumps that embody the powers of each Path. As always, relationship is paramount when it comes to Paths: the Triads (sets or triangles) of relationships are sources of immense spiritual insight and transformation.

The Path Triads

The Tree of Life is arranged in sets of three, such as the spheres or Emanations, which are in three sets of three (9), with a 10th unit for the totality of the nine.

The 22 Paths of the Tree also have Triad patterns, in several combinations that can be seen in figure 1. These Triads offer us much to meditate upon, and then to experience in Path working techniques.

The Stellar, Solar, and Lunar Path Triads (1/2/3) (4/5/6) (7/8/9).

The Three Pillars Triads: the three "verticals"(10/9/6/1) (8/5/3/1) (7/4/2/1). Note that these are not three triangles, but three sets of three Paths each.

The Three Wheels Triad: the three "horizontals"(7/8,5/4,3/2). Note this is not a triangle, but three concentric spheres, with the "horizontals" shown as a small part of each wheel.

The Triads of the Stars, or of Crossing the Abyss (6/3/2)(6/4/2)(6/5/3) (6/2/1) (6/3/1).

The Triads of the Sun, or radiant Triads (6/7/8) (6/5/8) (6/4/7) (6/7/9) (6/8/9).

The Triads of the Moon, or of Manifestation (7/8/10) (7/9/10) (8/9/10).

This is a lot simpler to follow in practice than to read about, though you can find all the Triads easily by examining figure 1. Before we can practice Path working, we need some information on the Paths and Path Triads. Let us begin with the primary Path Triads. To work with this set of concepts you should have a colored Tree of Life (*see Appendix 3*) and follow the diagrams referred to in the text.

For the later phases of Path working you will also need a set of Tarot trumps for this work, preferably the *Merlin*

Tarot[1] or the deck by A.E. Waite and P. Coleman Smith (known as the *Rider Waite Tarot*[2]). Both of these decks are attuned to the Western Qabalistic traditions, and have many inner contacts and powerful resonances. *The Merlin Tarot* is based on the Qabalah found in the medieval Merlin legends, the oldest known literary source for tarot images and Tree of Life cosmology.[3] The Merlin trumps are shown in figures 9 and 10.

Building Awareness of the Paths

The traditional method for Path working is deceptively simple: you sit or stand, and become aware of the Emanations (of the Path) on your right and left. You align with them, attune to them, and fill your awareness with them. The combined powers of the Emanations will propel you forward, over the bridge, into the consciousness of the Path. Thus, for the Path of the Sun, you attune to Beauty and Solar Light on one side, and Foundation and Lunar Light on the other. Build your sense of these two Emanations (6th and 9th) until it fills your awareness: feel them merge together in your body. Be Still, in the Beautiful Foundation.

To develop through this form of Path working, you should build your own key words for each Path. Some key phrases are included for each Path in the examples and brief outlines that follow, but build your own as a result of your Path working. At first you will write them down, but with practice you will be able to hold the *totality* of each Path within your memory not as a checklist, but as a living synthesis of the spiritual powers and concepts of each of the two Emanations of the Path.

This is the purest and most powerful form of Path working, and is likely to be the oldest form. At some later date, associated images were built up, preserved in oral tradition, and handed down from teacher to students. These were formalized in Wisdom tales, such as the adventures of Merlin in his journey from foolish boy to wise elder (in the *Vita Merlini* which includes descriptions of tarot trumps three centuries before the first picture cards were created). By the Renaissance period in Italy, such images became formalized as hand painted cards, which were the source of the later printed tarot decks.

It is worth discovering that Path working without Trumps produces "new" Path insights, while Path working with Trumps brings us into the collective Wisdom of the tradition. You should work with both methods.

Using the Trump Images

Once you have practiced all 22 Paths with the method described above, you can begin to add in the trump images for each Path. How is this done? Each trump image, each picture, is Before you in the layout of the Directions. The Emanations of the associated Path are on your Right and Left (do not worry about which Emanation is on which side: this will come to you intuitively, and you can experiment with crossovers, exchanging sides). The human world of consensuality, outer awareness, is Behind you.

To begin with, you can have a card in sight, on your meditation altar, and work with eyes open. When you know the trumps, you can work with or without a card, and work with eyes open or closed. The fusion of the Emanations (concepts and powers on your Right and Left) propels you along the Path (the trump image Before you) away from the outer world (Behind you).

This simple method will provide you with insights and inner transformations to last a lifetime and beyond, for many lifetimes.

The Path Triads described

There are three primary Path Triads, which, of themselves, encompass and include all other Paths. These other Paths are the secondary Path Triads, which we will explore later in this chapter.

The three primary Path Triads are as follows:

1. Lunar: the triangle of Paths between Emanations 9/8/7.
2. Solar: the triangle of Paths between Emanations 6/5/4.
3. Stellar: the triangle of Paths between Emanations 1/2/3.

The Lunar Path Triad

The lunar triangle comprises the relationship between the forces of Foundation/Moon, Scintillation/Mercury, and Exaltation/Venus.

The Paths that link each of the three spheres or Emanations together show these. Thus we have three primary Paths in this Path Triad:

1. Between Mercury and Venus, 8-7.
2. Between Moon and Mercury, 9-8.
3. Between Moon and Venus, 9-7.

Let us first examine, explore, and meditate upon what it is that the Paths mediate from the Emanations. In this exploration, the Paths are shown according to figure 12. You will see many books that describe another system, calling it the "traditional" numbering of the Paths. This is a reference to the layout and numbering system used by 19th century occultists in publication, which is not used in this book. We work instead with the more organic cosmological pattern, found the medieval Merlin texts, and in the Axis Mundi patterns of Renaissance tarot. This is the pattern that was taught to initiates who saw past the "blind" of the 19th century system, which was intentionally scrambled to test students. Nowadays a secretive obstructive approach (to the correct ordering of Paths) is redundant, but unfortunately the "traditional" order of the Paths is repeated frequently in publication.

1. Between Mercury and Venus: Scintillation, Brilliance, Glory and Exaltation, Ecstasy, Victory. Between thoughts and feelings, intellect and emotion. The driving power of our human existence, the cycle of our consciousness in daily life.

2. Between Moon and Mercury: Foundation and Glory. Between the life forces and bloodstream and the mind. Between the collective tribal dream world and ancestral Wisdom, and the individual analytical consciousness.

3. Between Moon and Venus: Foundation and Victory. Between the life forces and bloodstream and the feelings. Between the collective tribal dream world and ancestral Wisdom, and the individual emotions.

This Lunar Path Triad is demonstrated and mediated by Trumps of Fortune, Priest (magician), and Priestess.

The Path of Fortune, or the Wheel of Fortune is the first of Three Wheels (Fortune, Justice, Judgment) that encompass the Lunar, Solar, and Stellar Worlds. These are the three "horizontal" Paths on a standard Tree of Life. In fact, they are segments of three circles that encompass the entire Tree, as shown in the concentric spheres of figure 2. In all flat Tree of Life emblems, look for the three-dimensional pattern that they simplify. In this case, it is the three concentric spheres or Worlds, of Stars, Sun, Moon.

The Path of the Wheel of Fortune is the cycle of thoughts and feelings, highs and lows, exaltations and examinations, which is our daily life, and the cycle of a lifetime.

The Path of the Priest or Magus is the male mediator of the spiritual powers of the 8th Emanation, working with the powers of the 9th Emanation. The analytical and pattern making consciousness working with the deep roots of the lunar consciousness.

The Path of the Priestess is the female mediatrix of the spiritual powers of the 7th Emanation, working with the 9th, the emotional feeling and intuitive consciousness working with the deep roots of the lunar consciousness.

The Polarities of Priest and Priestess are not sexual stereotypes: they represent modes of consciousness and energy that flow through both male and female and encompass all living creatures that think and feel.

Observe and meditate upon how the lunar Path Triad has a pair that balances one another through the Foundation, and a third Path that represents the cycle of their powers. This pattern holds true also for the Solar and Stellar Path Triads.

The Solar Path Triad

The solar triangle comprises the relationship between the forces of Beauty/Sun, Severity/Mars, and Mercy/Jupiter.

The Paths that link each of the three spheres or Emanations together show these. Thus we have three primary Paths in this Path Triad:

1. Between Severity and Mercy, 5-4.
2. Between Beauty and Severity, 6-5.
3. Between Beauty and Mercy, 6-4.

Let us explore each Path in the Path Triad briefly:

1. Between Mars and Jupiter: Severity and
    Mercy, taking and giving, destroying and cre-
    ating, breaking down and building up, con-
    traction and expansion. This is usually a Path
    of cycles, both in the life forces of any living
    being, and in the cosmic forces of the solar
    system. If the balance tips too far toward
    Mercy or expansion, a corresponding force
    of Severity and contraction is triggered; if the
    balance tips too far towards Severity, a cor-
    responding power of Mercy is triggered. This
    cosmic Law is at the heart of all ritual magic,
    if it is rightly understood and worked with.
    Many of the forms used in advanced
    Qabalistic work are based on this pattern. In
    the day-to-day sense, our health and vitality
    is based on this same pattern. It is a source of
    primary meditation for anyone working with
    the Tree of Life.

2. Between Sun and Mars: Beauty, Balance, Har-
    mony, and Severity. This part of the Triad is
    about the forces of destruction working to-
    ward Balance. The connection between Mars
    and Sun, Severity and Harmony, is that of an
    extreme polarity and the center. This Path is
    the destroying arm of the 6th Emanation,
    while the 5th Emanation is its hand. This Path
    destroys patterns or forms in decline in or-
    der to bring Harmony. It is a Path of purifi-
    cation, especially of the breaking down of
    old patterns, forces, and forms, that must
    be recycled.

3. Between Sun and Jupiter: Harmony and Mercy. This part of the Triad is about the forces of creation and expansion working to bring Balance. This is the Path of polarity and center that Balances the Path between Emanations 5-6 described above. This is the creating or building arm of the 6th Emanation, while the 4th Emanation is its hand. This Path creates new potentials in order to bring Harmony. It is a Path of expansion, especially of compassion, and of strengthening new patterns, forces, and forms that must be built up and nourished.

This Solar Path Triad is demonstrated and mediated by the trumps of Justice, Blasted Tower, and Strength.

The Path of the Wheel of Justice: This wheel encompasses Fortune, which is within it, and devolves from it. The Wheel of Justice is the creative/destructive cycle of the solar forces: of the big picture rather than the Earthbound or humanocentric. The Trump of the goddess of Justice contains the emblems of this power: sword and chalice, scales of balance, the throne of power, and the veil behind the throne that hides the Abyss.

The Path of the Blasted Tower: This is the Path of purifying Fire, of the lightning bolt that blasts imbalanced patterns and forms away. While it may seem to be difficult if we are "on the receiving end," this Path breaks down in order to create anew. This is the power that destroys for harmonious ends. We can enter into this power willingly, which is one of the "secret" Paths of spiritual transformation, or receive it within the cycle of birth-death-rebirth.

The Path of Strength: This is the Path of nourishment and building power. It shows a maiden goddess gently subduing or holding a lion at peace. While the lion is the

198 ⚸   The Miracle Tree

wild power of the Sun, the goddess is that merciful aspect that keeps the lion calm. In our traditional tarot
trumps, this is one of several images that arise from the
ancient goddess Wisdom of our ancestors. The maiden
and the lion are the separate components of the destroy-
ing goddess (Durga in Hindu tradition), held in balance
to promote sustenance and strength. This is the Path of
peaceful balanced strength, not brute force.

The Stellar Path Triad

The stellar triangle comprises the relationship between
the forces of Understanding/Saturn, Wisdom/Neptune, and
TheCrown/Uranus.

The Paths that link each of the three spheres or Emanations together show these. Thus we have three primary
Paths in this Path Triad:

1. Between Understanding and Wisdom, 3-2
2. Between Wisdom and the Crown, 2-1
3. Between Understanding and the Crown, 3-1

Let us explore each Path in the Path Triad briefly:

1. Between Saturn and Neptune: Understanding and Wisdom. The interaction between the
   Deep Mother of Time and Space, and the Star
   Father of universal motion and energy. These
   are the polarities of Being, with the 3rd Emanation containing and drawing All into itself, and
   the 2nd Emanation declaring and issuing All out
   of itself.
2. Between Neptune and Uranus: Wisdom and
   Being, the Star Father and the Crown. The
   patterned Stars, and the Primum Mobile
   emerging from the Void of Unbeing. This Path

is the Path of One becoming Two, of universal expansion and primary movement out of stillness.

3. Between Saturn and Uranus: Understanding and Being, the Deep Mother and the Crown. The universal Vessel of Time and Space, within which the first movement of Being is contained, and out of which the manifest stellar patterns emerge. This is the Path of Three containing One, and of Three returning to One.

The Stellar Path Triad is demonstrated and mediated by the Trumps of Judgment, Innocent, and Hermit.

The Path of the Wheel of Judgment encompasses All. It is the perimeter or metaphysical boundary of the Stellar World, which contains within itself the Solar and Lunar Worlds, embodied by the Wheels of Justice and Fortune. These Three Wheels form another Path Triad, which is sometimes called the Three Thresholds or the Three Veils. The Trump of Judgment is usually propagandized in tarot to show the "last judgment" with the apocalyptic vision of an archangel calling the elect from their graves. In the *Merlin Tarot* we follow the apocalyptic vision in *The Prophecies of Merlin*, wherein the Weaver Goddess broods over the ocean of time and space, and closes the cycles of manifestation. See Appendix Four for this ancient source.

The Path of the Innocent embodies the primal spirit of Being emerging into stellar patterns. It is the universal equivalent of the New Born, having both innocence of experience, and primal eternal Wisdom simultaneously. In most tarot decks this trump is shown as the Hierophant or Pope, giving the spirit of the trump a worldly or materialized aspect. In the *Merlin Tarot* we follow older traditions, including descriptions in the Merlin texts themselves. The trump becomes the

Innocent, a young female, or possibly an androgynous being sitting upon the throne of power at the threshold of the universe. In some traditions Wisdom is feminine (Sophia). Here we have the idea of the polarized outward reaching universal power as ever-young, increasingly expanding into its "masculine" forms, which are the deities of the Star Father, and of the 4th Emanation, the Sky gods.

The Path of the Hermit: internalizes, and returns to the Source. While the Innocent/Hierophant flows out, the Hermit reaches in. This image, of a wise elder at the top of a high mountain, holds up the Lamp of Understanding for those who follow. The Hermit fuses Understanding and the Spirit, seeking a silent wordless formless truth that returns to the Source of All, the Crown of the Tree of Life. Thus it is the polar partner to the Innocent/ Hierophant.

The Vertical Triads

The vertical Triads are really the Off Planet Triads, for they extend our relativistic awareness through Moon, Sun, and Stars. The major vertical Triad is the Middle Pillar, merging the Emanations of Kingdom, Foundation, Beauty, and Crown (10/9/6/1). This Off Planet Triad comprises, as we might expect, the Paths of Moon (10-9), Sun (9-6), and Star (6-1), embodied by the tarot trumps of the same name.

10-9 Moon: Firm Foundation, Kingdom of Life, Moon and Earth.

9-6 Sun: Beautiful Foundation, Harmony of Life, Moon and Sun.

6-1 Star: Crown of Beauty: Being in Balance: Sun and Stars.

Balancing the Middle Pillar, or Axis Mundi (Pivot of the Worlds) are the Right and Left Hand Pillars. These are usually defined "as you look at the Tree," so the left hand is on your left, and the right hand on your right. These pillars are also Triads:

The Triad of Purification, Reduction, and Contraction

8-5 Guardian: Brilliant Severity, reason and discipline, Mercury and Mars.

5-3 Death: Severest Understanding, purifying within, Mars and Saturn.

3-2 Hermit: Crown of Understanding, withdrawing into Being, Saturn and Uranus.

Note: The Path 3-1, Hermit, is also in the Supernal Triad. It is mirrored in the polar opposite Path, that of 10-8, the Fool, Glory of Body, Brilliant Adventure, Mercury and Earth. So the Triad can also be 10-8, 5-3, 3-2. This sharing of Paths between Triads holds many profound insights in meditation. The Fool, at the beginning of the Journey of Life, and the Hermit, at the end, are one and the same.

The Triad of Growth, Increase, and Expansion

7-4 Empress: Exultant Mercy, generous feelings, Venus and Jupiter.

4-2 Emperor: Merciful Wisdom, boundless expansion, Neptune and Jupiter.

2-1 Innocent: Wise Being, Becoming universe, Neptune and Uranus.

Note: The Path 2-1, Innocent, is also in the Supernal Triad. It is mirrored in the polar opposite Path, that of 10-7, the universe or World, Ecstasy of Manifestation, Feeling Kingdom, Venus and Earth. The Innocent, primal Wisdom emerging from perfect Being, is the octave of the World of feeling and experience in manifestation.

Paths so far

Up to this point, we have explored 18 Paths: Fortune, Priestess, Magician/Justice, Strength, Tower/Justice, Hermit, Innocent/Moon, Sun, Star/Fool, Guardian, Death/World, Empress, Emperor. There remain four further Paths, Chariot/Lovers, and Hanged Man/Temperance. These four complete the sets of Triads of Sun and Stars.

The Lovers, 7-6, are within the Solar radiant Triad of 6-4, 4-7, 7-6. The Chariot, 8-6 is within the Solar radiant Triad of 6-5, 5-8, 8-6. Follow the basic Tree of Life, and figure 12 which has the trumps upon the Paths. The Radiant Paths are shown in figure 6.

7-6 The Lovers: Beautiful Ecstasy, Harmony of Feeling, Sun and Venus.

8-6 The Chariot: Harmonious Brilliance, Enlightened Reason, Sun and Mercury.

The Hanged Man, 6-3, is within the Stellar Crossing Triad of 6-3, 3-1, 1-6. This Triad of trumps and Paths crosses the Abyss, with a polarity that internalizes or goes into the Void. Temperance, 6-2, is within the Stellar Crossing Triad of 6-2, 2-1, 2-6. This Triad of trumps and Paths crosses the Abyss, with a polarity that externalizes and issues out of the Void.

6-3 Hanged Man: Beautiful Suspension, Harmonious Understanding, Sun and Saturn.

6-2 Temperance: Stellar Beauty, Wisdom of Harmony, Sun and Neptune.

Your task, as a developing Qabalist, is to explore the relationships of the Triads of Paths in meditation. And to work with the powers of each Path in Path working. If you follow the simple guidelines in this chapter, you will become familiar with the Paths in an organic and interactive manner, which will steadily transform your awareness and your subtle forces.

To conclude this outline of the Paths and Trumps, here are some meditative hints on the relationship between Paths, trumps, and the human body.

Paths, Trumps, and the Body

Once you have discovered the World Tree or Axis Mundi tarot trump patterns, you are attuning to the cosmic relationships embodied in the Paths of the Tree and the images behind tarot. It should always be remembered that tarot is not a set of cards: it is a set of highly interactive images that come from a cosmic vision. This vision, which is one of relationships, was giving rise to "tarot images" centuries before the first hand painted cards in Renaissance Italy[4], and formed the basis for the inner traditions handed down through the centuries. The vision itself is nothing more nor less than a statement of that which is present: the relationship between Earth, Moon, Sun and Stars, and how that relationship is mirrored in the natural forces of the solar system and Planet Earth, and in the human body/consciousness.

Just as the spheres or Emanations of the Tree of Life have a relationship to the polarities of the body and consciousness, so do the Paths. If you follow this simple summary in your meditations, it will bear valuable fruit.

The Three Wheels, Fortune, Justice, Judgment

Fortune: the hips and genitals. The Lunar Triad of the Tree.

Justice: the heart and lungs, or across the upper body. The Solar Triad of the Tree. Justice is associated with the powers of the right and left hand, and it can move downwards in the Lunar zone, or upwards into the stellar zone.

Judgment: above the right and left shoulders: the Stellar or Supernal Triad of the Tree.

These three Paths and associated trump images are located horizontally across the body, with the extreme poles of their power on the right and left. But you may also sense them as circles around the body: at the level of hips, heart, and head. When you do so, they are part of the sphere of your consciousness and energy.

Another way to work with these three Paths is to meditate upon them as the Three Rings that make the dynamics of your sphere of Being.

1. Judgment is the ring that surrounds us vertically, passing from before us to behind us. Thus it embodies, in miniature, the passage of any one life, from that which is before us at birth, to that which is behind us at death.
2. Justice is the ring that surrounds us laterally, rotating from right to left and left to right. It embodies the balance and cycles of creative and destructive forces during our lifetime.
3. Fortune is the horizontal ring, the wheel of the Life, the seasons, the day, the moods, the thoughts, the biological cycles.

In many branches of Qabalah the Three Rings have a supernal role, during the origination of the universe. At this level they are Time (Judgment, Wisdom/Understanding, the poles of diffusion and attraction), Space (Justice, Severity/ Mercy, or the poles of polarity or difference), and Events or Movement (Fortune, Glory and Victory, or the poles of ceaseless interaction).

Little wonder, therefore, that our every action, standing, walking, sitting, is a mirror of the cosmic forces of the Tree of Life. It is this mirroring or harmonic principle that enables the many *forms* of Qabalistic practice to work so strongly through the body.

Chapter 8

The Tree of
Life and Death

You cannot have life without death. This simple truth is the entire truth of the Tree of Life. It is inevitably the Tree of Life and Death, the Tree of Possibilities. There are as many death forces on the Tree as there are life forces. Unfortunately for us, the idea of death is laden with denials and fears. Think of this denial of death; meditate upon it, as nothing more than a cultural aberration.

You already know about death, you have died many times, just as you have been born many times. Those memories are present within you, and death is a normal everyday experience. Consider and meditate upon the fact that your body dies ceaselessly. Just as cells die and are regenerated, we live and die second by second through our lives. This cellular process is the normal pattern and we are not exempt from it. All that changes is the time-cycle. There is a relative difference between your life span and that of your cells, just as there is a difference between your life and that of the Sun.

One third of the Emanations on the Tree are those that destroy, draw in, and restrict, and one third are those that create, give out, and expand. The other third, for everything on the Tree is in Triads, consists of those that are in balance. This balance is not static, but dynamic.

In this chapter we will explore the way in which human death and rebirth is shown upon the Tree of Life. Through working with the Tree, we can enter death in a manner that is conscious and graceful, and your Qabalistic training in the various forms will alter many of the "automatic" processes that occur during death and rebirth. The result of this is a heightened awareness and a greater continuity of memory.

Memory, Sleep, and Death

Both sleep and death are associated with memory. Both cross between different states of consciousness, different physical states, and both require loss of memory. Let us examine this further, as the Tree of Life maps much of this process, and also provides us with means not only to understand, but also to transform the rhythms of sleep and death.

When we sleep, we forget the outer world and enter the dream world. When we wake, we forget our dreams but our memory of the outer world returns. Somewhere, the storehouse of deep memory bridges across both. In dreams we have confused and sometimes clear intimations of the connections between inner and outer worlds.

There are three classes of dream:

1. Most dreams are reworkings of day-to-day concerns, and are a process of mental and emotional digestion and elimination.

2. Some declare deeper issues or long term patterns in the individual that resonate until they are resolved or harmonized.

3. A third class of dreams involves spiritual perception, and this has a different quality than the first two.

When we die, we forget the outer world as we progressively enter the inner world. When we are born we forget the inner world, and arrive with little memory of our previous lives. Somewhere, the storehouse of deep memory bridges across both. Often dreams of the third class bridge across lives to indicate the deeper reality of our Being. Sometimes dreams of the second class will indicate deep patterns that are carried from life to life until they are resolved or until they simply fade away.

On the Tree, the world of sleep and dreams is found on the other side of the first bridge that we cross. Sometimes this is called "lesser crossing of the Abyss." This is our daily crossing from one state of consciousness to another, to and fro, and is via the Path of The Moon. This same Path is taken at birth and at death, between the 10th and 9th Emanations, the Kingdom and Foundation, the outer manifest world and the inner world of potentials.

We do not always stop at the Moon, of course. Our dreams will circulate around the Wheel of Fortune until we awaken, encompassing our thoughts (8th Emanation) our feelings (7th), and our generative sexual forces (9th). As you might think, from the connection between our regular consciousness and the Wheel of Fortune, our sleep and dream cycle has a relationship to the planetary rotation. So the Qabalist should try to sleep in rhythm with the Sun, especially with the early sunrise. This is why, in spiritual and monastic disciplines, the waking at or before dawn is given significance.

Death is the greater crossing of the Abyss, the process whereby our manifest body (10th Emanation) and the 9 Emanations, *separate from one another in terms of our relative consciousness.* Death crosses exactly the same bridge as Sleep, but goes further on.

When we die, our fusion of mind/emotions/desires separates from the physical body. Thus, for a certain length of time, we are within the Wheel of Fortune, but without the means of expression (the Body), and we cannot return to the outer world. This is the classic *post mortem* state that is described by mediums and channelers, and can be a pastiche or mimicry of the cultural world that the individual has left behind. It is a realm in which habit and imagination rule jointly. Habit, established through a lifetime, remains as a temporary binding force, while imagination enables the individual to be mobile.

Gradually, the personality begins to dissolve. It no longer has the bodily sustenance, and cannot satisfy the desires of the habits through the imagination. At this point, many of us are drawn back to the outer life and are reborn. Our previous personality is forgotten, but we retain a pattern of habits and desires, which is shown in the natal chart, and in the tendencies and preferences that soon show in the developing child. These tendencies can, and do, change and develop, and they never bind us.

If the dead man or woman has done some spiritual work during life, they can focus the imagination on other conditions, rather than backwards to the outer world. In the orthodox religions, these conditions are the heavenly realms (or depending on your tradition, other spiritual dimensions). Such artificial dimensions are maintained by a group soul, and can form a refuge (for a while) in which the individual soul rests. But they are not permanent.

If we make this transition in a more enlightened manner, with imagination triumphant (7th Emanation) over habit, we move away from our fading ties to the outer world, toward the deeper inner worlds. Or if you are looking at a standard Tree of Life, we cross into the Solar World. When we do so, we forget much of the recent life, and the habits of the personality are shed like old rags that have been outworn.

So the individual has crossed the Abyss (which is nothing more than the relative distance between one state of Being and another) from the Lunar World, into the Solar World.

Here we come under the Wheel of Justice, which is why the "weighing of the soul" is a theme in the ancient religions and Mysteries. Most of us come back into rebirth, cleansed, radiant, and ready for the new life. On the way back through the Lunar World, we will collect certain patterns of consciousness that imprint the life. These are shown in the natal chart, and in the deeper talents, skills, and preferences of the developing child and adult.

These patterns include 9th Emanation ancestral tendencies (the genetic line), mental and emotional potentials, 7th and 8th Emanations, and all shape up as the outer body, in the 10th—the Kingdom.

A few individuals go further, and cross the Abyss into the Stellar World, the supernal spheres of the Tree. Such individuals do not return to birth.

At a deeper level, the long-term result is that we grow beyond physical expression in this world of Earth, and this teaching is a major part of the tradition. The innerworld saints, wise men and women, mentors, those who work with us, but live in spiritual dimensions, are found at that place on the Tree of Life that is beyond the cycle of Death and Rebirth, beyond the Wheel of Fortune.

Death and the Three Wheels

Think of the Three Wheels (Fortune, Justice, and Judgment) as three modes of consciousness, three ways of Being. Fortune, which is the wheel that turns at high speed creating the changes of the thoughts, emotions, and the interactions that we experience in any lifetime, is our regular mode of consciousness. We live within the turning of the Wheel of Fortune.

But this Wheel is within another wheel, which turns more slowly: the Wheel of Justice. It is when we touch upon the power of Justice that we die, and are reborn. Justice also brings the longer-term death and rebirth, or change of cycles, in the solar and planetary world. Many of the environmental disruptions that we experience at present are manifestations of the power of Justice, whereby the Planet seeks to bring unbalanced patterns back into harmony again. This Adjustment principle works, in the larger sense, with each life and death and rebirth that we undergo.

And Justice is within another wheel, the cosmic wheel of Judgment, which moves slowly through millenniums. This all-encompassing wheel turns the universe through its own cycles of birth, death, and rebirth. Physically, this is revealed to us as the death and birth of the Stars, but in terms of consciousness, it is the deep Understanding and Wisdom that encompasses All.

During our everyday life, and any one life in this world, we are usually within the Wheel of Fortune. This is the wheel that is expressed in the interactions of your birth chart. Not the wheel that creates the patterns or the matrix of the chart, but the cycle of interactions and changes that you live through day by day, year by year.

The Wheel of Justice is the power that creates the matrix of the chart, stamping it, so to speak, at the time of birth. In fact, this matrix is already being created before we are born, and is finalized at birth. It is a set of potentials in a pattern of interaction: it is Adjusted (Justice) with each lifetime.

The Wheel of Judgment originates the spiritual forces that are expressed through the Planets, signs, and houses in your natal chart. Its influence will also show in the long term planetary interactions that have gained a lot of popular attention in recent years: those of Saturn, Uranus, Pluto, and Neptune.

Working with the Tree of Life, we may enter into one of the greatest miracles that spiritual life can offer. Instead being under the wheels, we can discover that we are within them, and that we have a conscious part to play in the patterns.

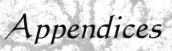

Appendices

Appendix A

Work plans and programs: using the forms

General rules

1. Do the forms in the order in which they are set out in each chapter. Do not jump into the later forms without practicing the preceding forms. Practice each form for not less than 10 minutes, not more than 20 minutes. Brief focused work is better than long strenuous sessions. Spending 10 minutes per day on any one form is ample.

    Time off: it is better to work through a longer cycle and then take a week off, rather than having days off during any one week.

2. Initially it is helpful to draw up a simple calendar, to remind yourself to do a short daily session with your current form. Try to do this at the same time each day.

The Miracle Tree

Forms (Chapters 1-6)

1. Practice each form for 10 days before going on to the next form. Then, of course, stay with them for the many years of inner transformation and insight that they will bring! You can do more than one 10-day cycle on any one form, as many as you wish, before moving on to the next.

2. In any 10-day cycle, start to bring in the next form around day 6, and practice it on days 6, 8, and 10. Day 10 becomes day 1 of the new 10-day cycle with the new form.

3. After six 10-day cycles (60 days of forms, or two lunar periods), take a full 10 days off: no meditations of any sort.

Some of the forms have further suggestions for work cycles, and eventually you will want to build your own patterns. The work with Paths and Trumps, for example (Chapter 7) requires a longer-term cycle of initial meditations and observations, before entering into Path workings themselves.

Path workings (Chapter 7)

1. As there are 22 Paths, you can follow a three-week cycle of one Path per day, initially, with two Paths on the first/last day of the cycle. After this, take one week off from Paths, but resume work with the basic forms day by day during that week. At the end of this whole month (three weeks of Paths, one week of basic forms), take a week off entirely.

2. Path workings in Triads. Once you have completed some three-week cycles with the Paths,

start to work with the Triads, one Triad per day. Work out your own cycle of Paths on specific days for this: you can encompass the entire Tree as Path Triads in 14 days. At the end of the cycle, take one week off from all Qabalistic work.

Vacations and traveling

1. During vacations, practice the walking forms. Let your practices become part of the vacation.
2. During travel, when you are restricted by long hours on the plane, train, bus, or car, practice the visionary forms (but not if you are driving). Travel time can also be used for your basic memory of the Emanations, Paths, and trumps of the Tree of Life. Sit quietly and build the Tree in your imagination: the Emanations, the Paths, the colors, the trumps, the angels, and archangels.

Follow this memory-meditation with alignments to the body: the Lunar, Solar, and Stellar Worlds in the lower, middle, and upper zones of the body.

Mundane tasks

1. Practice forms such as the Rising Light, and Walking Participation while you are undertaking mundane tasks: cleaning the yard, washing the dishes, anything that involves physical work can be attuned to these forms.

Sleep and Notes or Journals

1. Form a clear intention each night as you go to sleep to work with the form or Path that you have chosen for that day. Go into meditation

by being Still, using the Stillness form, then form your intention to pursue the daily form or Path or Triad during sleep. If you wish, make notes in the morning.

2. Keep a journal of your work with the Tree of Life. But remember that the Journal is not an end in itself. Ultimately the experiences live in you, not in your notes.

Appendix B

The Story of Er (Qabalistic tradition within Plato's *Republic*)

These extracts are based on the 19th century translation by Benjamin Jowett, 1871.

The Death Vision of Er

The tale of a hero, Er the son of Armenius, a Pamphylian by birth. He was slain in battle, and 10 days afterwards, when the bodies of the dead were taken up already in a state of corruption, his body was found unaffected by decay, and carried away home to be buried. And on the twelfth day, as he was lying on the funeral pile, he returned to life and told them what he had seen in the other world. He said that when his soul left the body he went on a journey with a great company, and that they came to a mysterious place at which there were two openings in the Earth; they were near together, and over against them were two other openings in the heaven above. In the intermediate space there were judges seated, who commanded the just, after they had given judgment on them

221

and had bound their sentences in front of them, to ascend by the heavenly way on the right hand; and in like manner the unjust were bidden by them to descend by the lower way on the left hand; these also bore the symbols of their deeds but fastened on their backs. He drew near, and they told him that he was to be the messenger who would carry the report of the other world to men, and they bade him hear and see all that was to be heard and seen in that place. Then he beheld and saw on one side the souls departing at either opening of heaven and Earth when sentence had been given on them; and at the two other openings other souls, some ascending out of the Earth dusty and worn with travel, some descending out of heaven clean and bright. And arriving ever and anon they seemed to have come from a long journey, and they went forth with gladness into the meadow, where they encamped as at a festival; and those who knew one another embraced and conversed, the souls which came from Earth curiously inquiring about the things above, and the souls which came from heaven about the things beneath. And they told one another of what had happened by the way, those from below weeping and sorrowing at the remembrance of the things which they had endured and seen in their journey beneath the Earth (now the journey lasted a thousand years), while those from above were describing heavenly delights and visions of inconceivable beauty.

The Vision of the Solar Proportions (or Tree of Life)

Now when the spirits which were in the meadow had tarried seven days, on the eighth they were obliged to proceed on their journey, and, on the fourth day after, he said that they came to a place where they could see from above a line of light, straight as a column, extending right through the whole heaven and through the Earth, in color resembling the rainbow, only brighter and purer; another day's journey brought them to the place, and there, in the midst of the light, they saw the ends of the chains of heaven let down from above: for this light is the belt of heaven, and holds together the circle of the universe, like the under-girders of a trireme. From these ends is extended the spindle of the goddess of Necessity, on which all the revolutions turn. The shaft and hook of this spindle are made of steel, and the whorl is made partly of steel and also partly of other materials. Now the whorl is in form like the whorl used on Earth; and the description of it implied that there is one large hollow whorl which is quite scooped out, and into this is fitted another lesser one, and another, and another, and four others, making eight in all, like vessels which fit into one another; the whorls show their edges on the upper side, and on their lower side all together form one continuous whorl. This is pierced by the spindle, which is driven home through the center of the eighth. The first and outermost whorl has the rim broadest, and the seven inner whorls are narrower, in the following proportions— the sixth is next to the first in size, the fourth next to the sixth; then comes the eighth; the seventh is fifth, the fifth is sixth, the third is seventh, last and eighth comes the second. The largest [of fixed Stars] is spangled, and the seventh [or Sun] is brightest; the eighth [or Moon] colored by the reflected light of the seventh; the second and fifth [Saturn and Mercury] are in color like one another, and yellower than the preceding; the third [Venus] has the whitest light; the fourth [Mars] is reddish; the sixth [Jupiter] is in whiteness second. Now the whole spindle has the same motion; but, as the whole revolves in one direction, the seven inner circles move slowly in the other, and of these the swiftest is the eighth; next in swiftness are the seventh, sixth, and fifth, which move together; third in swiftness appeared to move according to the law of this reversed motion the fourth; the third appeared fourth and the second fifth. The spindle turns on the knees of the goddess of Necessity; and on the upper surface of each circle is a siren, who goes round with them, hymning a single tone or note. The eight together form one harmony; and round about, at equal intervals there is another band, three in number, each sitting upon her throne: these are the Fates, daughters of the goddess of Necessity, who are clothed in white robes and have chaplets upon their heads, Lachesis and Clotho and Atropos, who accompany with their voices the harmony of the sirens—Lachesis singing of the past, Clotho of the present, Atropos of the future; Clotho from time to time assisting with a touch of her right hand the revolution of the outer circle of the whorl or spindle, and Atropos with her left hand touching and guiding the inner ones, and Lachesis laying hold of either in turn, first with one hand and then with the other.

Choosing the pattern of life prior to rebirth

When Er and the spirits arrived, their duty was to go at once to Lachesis; but first of all there came a prophet who arranged them in order; then he took from the knees of Lachesis lots and samples of lives, and having mounted a high pulpit, spoke as follows: "Hear the word of Lachesis, the daughter of Necessity. Mortal souls, behold a new cycle of life and mortality. Your life spirit will not be allotted to you, but you choose your life spirit; and let him who draws the first lot have the first choice, and the life which he chooses shall be his destiny. Virtue is free, and as a man honors or dishonors her he will have more or less of her; the responsibility is with the chooser—Divine Wisdom is justified." When the prophet had thus spoken he scattered lots randomly among them all, and each of them took up the lot which fell near him, all but Er himself and each as he took his lot perceived the number which he had obtained. Then the prophet placed on the ground before them the samples of lives; and there were many more lives than the souls present, and they were of all sorts. There were lives of every animal and of man in every condition. And there were tyrannies among them, some lasting out the tyrant's life, others which broke off in the middle and came to an end in poverty and exile and beggary; and there were lives of famous men, some who were famous for their form and beauty as well as for their strength and success in games, or, again, for their birth and the qualities of their ancestors; and some who were the reverse of famous for the opposite qualities...

The souls cross the Abyss into rebirth

All the souls had now chosen their lives, and they went in the order of their choice to Lachesis, who sent with them the life-spirit whom they had severally chosen, to be the guardian of their lives and the fulfiller of the choice: this genius led the souls first to Clotho, and drew them within the revolution of the spindle impelled by her hand, thus ratifying the destiny of each; and then, when they were fastened to this, carried them to Atropos, who spun the threads and made them irreversible, whence without turning round they passed beneath the throne of Necessity and when they had all passed, they marched on in a scorching heat to the plain of Forgetfulness, which was a barren waste destitute of trees and verdure; and then towards evening they encamped by the river of Forgetfulness, whose Water no vessel can hold; of this they were all obliged to drink a certain quantity, and those who were not saved by Wisdom drank more than was necessary; and each one as he drank forgot all things. Now after they had gone to rest, about the middle of the night there was a thunderstorm and earthquake, and then in an instant they were driven upwards in all manner of ways to their birth, like Stars shooting. He himself was hindered from drinking the Water. But in what manner or by what means he returned to the body he could not say; only, in the morning, awaking suddenly, he found himself lying on the pyre.

Appendix C

The Colors of the Tree of Life

One of the main exercises for working with the Tree of Life is to draw and color a Tree for your own meditations. It is important that you draw and color this yourself, rather than buy a commercial print. The act of creating your own Tree gives it a magical resonance that you cannot obtain with a ready-made print. Traditionally this "training Tree" is hung on the wall behind your meditation altar, and is used for meditation with eyes open.

You can begin by drawing or tracing over the main Tree in our figure 1. Ideally your own Tree should be about twice as big. Leave the Emanations/spheres blank, as they are going to be colored with the primary colors of the Tree of Life.

In this summary, some meditative concepts are given for each color. As you paint or ink your Tree of Life, meditate upon the forces of each sphere/Emanation: if nothing else use the simple concepts of this summary. Later you will build up the subtle forces of your external Tree image through your Qabalistic meditations, when you sit with eyes open and explore the Emanations and Paths.

Here are the colors of the Tree, first the spectrum of colors (white, black, blue, red, green, orange, violet, brown) then the secondary colors of the planetary metals. You might wish to color a second Tree with the metallic hues.

1. Clear, or without color: Traditionally this sphere is left untinted, for it is the circle that is its "color," not whatever is contained by it.
2. Swirling silver gray: The color of Stars.
3. Deep black: No Light, but Understanding by deep touch and intuition. Can also be the color of lead.
4. Sky blue: The color of a clear dawn. Radiant blue is associated with Compassion. Can also be the brightness of tin.
5. Blood red: The purifying power of the goddess of Severity. Can also be metallic red.
6. Golden yellow: The color of the Sun.
7. Verdant green: The spring green of flourishing Nature. Can also be copper colored.
8. Bright orange: A vibrant "loud" color. Can also be mercurial silver.
9. Deep violet: Can also be the soft white pearly Light of moonlight.
10. A circle of rainbow colors: Alternatively: Black (North), Sea green (West), Red (South), Blue (East). Or: Black, Brown, Russet, Olive, the four "earthy" colors.

Colors for the Paths

Path colors are extensions of the primary colors of each Emanation or sphere. For example, the Path between Sun and Jupiter (6-4, Beauty and Mercy) would be golden yellow as it is emitted from the 6th Emanation, and sky blue from the 4th: in the center of the Path they will merge, and you may wish to have rays of each color reaching along the Path, one inside the other, for a short space after the merging in the middle. If you color a Tree according to this method, you will have a powerful meditational icon with radiant color patterns that stimulate inner vision and contemplation.

Always remember that the colors of the Tree of Life are not "symbolic," they embody the forces of the Emanations.

Appendix D

Extracts from The Merlin Texts, Qabalistic Material in the 12th Century *Prophecies of Merlin*

By the time you read this Appendix, you will be familiar with much of the basic terminology of the Tree of Life and demystified Qabalah. Once you have practiced some of the forms in this book, you will find many deep insights in these extracts from ancient verses. They are offered here as examples of Qabalistic imagery in ancient Western tradition, and they provide a fruitful set of meditations in their own right. For a detailed edition of the Merlin texts, see *Merlin, The Prophetic Vision and Mystic Life*, R J Stewart, Penguin Arkana.

The Vision of the Three Springs

These verses (from the *Prophecies*) include a vision of the goddess of the Land, and a practical teaching about breath and subtle energies. This is a typical traditional Wisdom-carrying vision, reminding us of material in classic Qabalah from various traditions and sources. It is likely

to be the remnant of a Wisdom teaching and vision pre-
serve in bardic (Welsh druidic) poetry.

> 42 *Three springs shall break forth in the city of Win-
> chester, whose rivulets shall divide the island into
> three parts. Whoever shall drink of the first, shall
> enjoy long life and never be afflicted with sickness.
> He that shall drink of the second, shall die of hun-
> ger and paleness and horror shall sit upon his coun-
> tenance.*

> 43 *He that shall drink of the third, shall be surprised
> with sudden death, neither shall his body be capable
> of burial. Those that are willing to escape so vora-
> cious a death, will endeavor to bide it with several
> coverings, but whatever bulk shall be laid upon it,
> shall receive the form of another body. For Earth
> shall be turned into stones; stones into Water; wood
> into ashes; ashes into Water, if cast over it.*

The Three Springs correspond to Life, Desire, and
Death. The first is the Clear or White Stream, the second
is the Red Stream, and the third is the Black Stream. The
desire to escape death, associated with the third Black
Stream, results in a cycle of elemental transformations:
Earth/stones/Water/wood (burnt by Fire)/ashes. This refers to the cycle of manifestation and rebirth of all forms,
all energies, and all beings. When we are newly born, the
White Stream is strongest within us. As we mature, the
Red Stream becomes the strongest. In maturity and old
age, the Black Stream is prevalent. The streams are a model
of the vital energies, the blood, and the body (Life force,
blood stream, form-building, and eliminatory systems).
On the Tree of Life these Streams are reflections, in the
Kingdom, of the Supernal Triad. The colors have specific

connections: Black to the 3rd Emanation, Red to the 5th, and White to the 2nd Emanation.

> 44 *A maiden shall be sent from the gathering place in the ancient forest, to administer a cure. Once she has practiced her oracular arts, she shall dry up the poisonous fountains by breathing upon them. After this, she shall refresh herself with the wholesome fountain, and shall bear in her right hand the forests of the North, and in her left hand the buttressed forts of London.*

Next comes a vision of the goddess of the Land. She appears as a virgin (maiden) out of the ancient forest, and breathes upon the two "poisonous" streams, the Red and the Black. She is the source of prophecy, for before breathing, she practices "oracular arts." Such imagery is often associated with wells, springs, and fountains in Celtic tradition. As they rise from the UnderWorld, they carry within them the visions of potential future patterns. After drinking from the wholesome (White) fountain, the goddess grows to full size, she is the Land: in one hand the forests of Caledon (the North) and in the other the city of the South (London). This is the goddess associated with the Kingdom, or 10th Emanation, the Land. But she is also a reflection or octave of the Great goddess, who encompasses Time and Space, the power of the 3rd Emanation.

> 45 *Wherever she shall go, she shall make sulfurous steps, which shall smoke with a double flame. That smoke shall rouse up the Ruteni, and shall make food for the inhabitants of the deep sea. Tears of compassion will overflow her eyes, and she shall fill the island with dreadful cries.*

The smoking footsteps of the goddess are found in various traditions, wherein images of deities are shown or described as having flames erupting where they touch the ground. The flames denote the inherent power of the deity. The smoke arouses ancestral memory, symbolized by the old tribal name of the Ruteni. Making food for the inhabitants of the deep sea, and the association with sulfur reminds us that life begins in the ocean depths, where the volcanic fires merge with deep waters, and primal life forms are generated. The goddess, now reaching from one end of the Land to the other, from North to South, has one foot on the land and one in the depths of the Sea. Her compassion flows out as tears. This image is strikingly similar to the tarot trump of Temperance. This trump represents the Path that crosses the Abyss between the universal ocean of Stars, and our specific Solar World (and Earth World within the Solar World).

46 *She shall be killed by a hart with ten branches, four of which shall bear golden diadems; but the other six shall be turned into the horns of oxen, whose hideous bellowing shall arouse the three islands of Britain.*

The next image is of a stag or hart with 10 branches (antlers). This is a power emblem. The stag is typically one of the power animals in Celtic tradition, and is closely associated with Merlin (along with the Wolf, the Pig, and the Crow). The upper four branches bear golden Crowns (diadems). These are the equivalent of the higher spheres on the Tree of Life, representing spiritual and solar forces. The lower six are earthier, appearing as the horns of oxen. The Ox is the traditional creature of the element of Earth: driving or turning the mill of power. The ancient sacred sign of the Swastika (in Hindu symbolism from India, not the reversed emblem of Nazism) is made from the horns of four oxen, turning a grinding mill, as seen from above. They symbolize the Elements and the Directions, the Wheel of Life. Though the verses state that the maiden is killed by the Stag, this sequence represents the mediation of elemental forces, from the realm of deity outward into nature: from the goddess, through the Three Streams, and out into manifestation, form, living creatures, and interaction. As always in the *Prophecies*, the interaction is dramatically symbolized by conflict, as in the next verses.

Inversion of Natural Order: Heralding Merlin's Apocalyptic Vision of the Goddess Ariadne

87 *From them shall the Stars turn away their faces, and confound their usual course. Corn will wither at their malign aspects, and there shall fall no dew from Heaven...*

88a *Root and branch shall change places, and the newness of the thing shall pass as a miracle.*

88b *The brightness of the Sun shall fade at the amber of Mercury, and horror shall seize the beholders. Stilbon of Arcadia shall change his shield; the Helmet of Mars shall call Venus.*

The inversion of root and branch is a potent image, and is similar to those found in various spiritual traditions that work with the Tree of Life, the World Tree, and the powers of the UnderWorld. Hidden depths come to the surface. That which was below becomes above, that which was above becomes below. In the UnderWorld traditions, this type of imagery, at its most profound level, refers to an exchange between the spiritual powers deep within our Planet, and those of the Solar System and other Stars.

In August of 1999 there was a long and powerful Mercury retrograde, followed by an eclipse of the Sun. These astrological/astronomical patterns marked the opening phase of a series that occurs, and is still occurring now (year 2002 C.E. and subsequent years) during the transition between the 20th and 21st centuries (c.e.). The Christian calendar millennium synchronizes with these transitional patterns, but the changes themselves are not defined by a Christian calendar, for they are cosmic in nature.

> 89 *The Helmet of Mars shall make a shadow and the rage of Mercury shall exceed its orbit. Iron Orion shall unsheathe his sword; the marine Phoebus shall torment the clouds. Jupiter shall go out of his lawful Paths; and Venus forsake her appointed circuits.*

This verse refers to planetary and stellar forces of change, and their impact upon our Planet. Orion is traditionally associated with storms, and "the marine Phoebus" is a poetic phrase describing Orion. Profound weather changes and increasing storms, such as the El Nino effect, are hallmarks of the close of the 20th century, and will continue to grow in the 21st.

> 90 *The malignity of the Star Saturn shall fall down in rain, and slay mankind with a crooked sickle. The Twelve Houses of the Stars shall lament the ir-regular excursions of their inmates.*

Poisonous rain is another feature of the 20th century, due to industrial and nuclear pollution. Saturn is a force of long-term change, slow and deep. Lead, the metal of Saturn, is associated with the poisons typical to 20th century pollution, especially lead and arsenic from the millions of internal combustion engines in motor vehicles. The lament of the Twelve Houses of the Stars marks the beginning of a cosmic and terrestrial shift. The Stars and Planets no longer follow their regular patterns in the sky. This can only occur if the relative position of our Planet Earth changes: the observed patterns are a relativistic effect as seen from Earth. If the Planet changes its position in orbit, the old patterns will no longer show in the night sky. This theme is developed in the following verses.

> 91 *The Gemini shall omit their usual embrace, and will call the Urn (Aquarius) to the fountains. The Scales of Libra shall hang awry, till Aries puts his crooked horns under them. The tail of Scorpio shall produce lightning, and Cancer quarrel with the Sun. Virgo shall mount upon the back of Sagittarius, and darken her Virgin flowers.*

The Signs are described as breaking away from their customary functions, creating disruption and chaos.

> 92 *The Chariot of the Moon shall disorder the Zodiac, and the Pleiades break forth into weeping. No offices of Janus shall return hereafter, but his gate being shut shall lie hid in the chinks of Ariadne.*

(alternative translation)

> 92 *The Chariot of the Moon shall disturb the Zodiac, and the Pleiades shall burst into tears and lamentations. None hereafter shall return to his wonted duty, but Ariadne shall lie hidden within the closed gateways of her sea-girt headland.*

(alternative translation)

With this verse we come to the heart of the Apocalyptic vision. The Chariot of the Moon refers to the cycle of the Lunar Nodes, which were considered of major importance in early astrology. The pattern of the Lunar Nodes forms a serpentine shape when mapped through the Signs and Houses. Nowadays the Dragon's Head and Tail are still used in modern astrology. The Pleiades are the celestial markers of the Seasons: the seasonal movement of this constellation was, and still is, observed in both northern and southern hemispheres. In May, the Pleiades mark the beginning of summer, in November; they mark the beginning of winter. They are also associated with birth and death: the May fertility festivals and the early November death festivals (Halloween). In the southern hemisphere, the seasons and festivals are reversed.

Janus (the god of crossroads and the Gatekeeper) is the power of transition and of choices at times of change. The month of January is named after this classical deity, who has either two faces (looking to the past and the future) or sometimes four faces (one for each of the Four Directions). Suddenly the Gate is closed, and the goddess Ariadne withdraws her creation. Ariadne is the spider or Weaver goddess. Geoffrey of Monmouth may have heard, or had before him as text, the Welsh goddess-name Arianrhod (Great Queen of the Wheel, sometimes translated as "silver-wheel"). In either case, classical or Welsh, the goddess is the same. She is the Weaver goddess who creates the Wheel of the Stars, and so the Wheel of Life. In Plato (Republic) this goddess is called Arete, which means necessity or virtue. She is described as twirling a distaff, from which the orbits of our solar system spin upon her colored threads.

Lewis Thorpe, the most recent translator of Geoffrey's History of the British Kings (Penguin Classics series), translates verse 92 as follows: *92 'None of these shall return to the duty expected of it. (Referring to the Planets and Signs) Ariadne will shut its door and be hidden within the enclosing cloud banks.'*

> 93 *The seas shall rise up in the twinkling of an eye, and the dust of the Ancients be restored. The winds shall fight together with a dreadful blast, and their Sound shall reach to the Stars.*

Is the final act of Apocalypse. The seas rising up may be interpreted as planetary seas, at first, flooding the lands as a result of the planetary shift of position. But they are also the seas of time, space, and Stars. The arousal of the Ancestors is the pagan version of a theme later adapted by the early Christians. At the Last Judgment, the archangel Gabriel, who is Regent of the West, the Moon, and the seas, summons the souls. This the tarot Trump of Judgment, which embodies the Wheel of Judgment, or the fusion of Understanding and Wisdom, the 3rd and 2nd Emanations. This is the Stellar World, encompassing all Time, Space, and Events. The sound of the winds coming together reaches to the Stars. This image derives from the tradition of the Four Winds of the World, the Four Directions. These are mundane reflections or manifestations of the Four Primary Powers, the phases of the Divine Word of Being. This verse should remind us that, with our technology, we "hear" the energies of distant Stars, even those that no longer exist.

We may think of this vision as working at different levels. It can be interpreted as a physical planetary event of major proportions, such as has happened in the past more than once. Many of the preliminary signs, such as weather changes, specific astrological patterns, and events in human culture, have already occurred. Like the Mayan and Hopi prophecies, the Prophecies of Merlin predict major changes and the end of a cycle sometime in the 21st century. The Apocalypse also refers to an inner or spiritual revolution, freeing the individual from the habitual patterns of the Wheel of Fortune, the Wheel of Life. The Wheel (of the goddess Ariadne/Arianrhod) is manifest through each of us in our natal chart, the birth chart found by astrological calculation. There is a further collective implication, for humanity as a race of beings, as part of the planetary collective and the Planetary Being. The 21st century is the time period in which major changes will become apparent, and the world will be transformed.

To conclude our extract and short commentary on the Apocalypse of Merlin: this material is within the genre of prophetic, Qabalistic, and apocalyptic poems, visions, or fragments, that were gradually enshrined as texts, over several centuries. The Merlin texts are not dogma, but examples of how the imagery, Qabalistic concepts, and visionary and prophetic themes, were widespread in the ancestral cultures. More specifically, the Merlin texts are one of the substantial proofs of an enduring third stream of Qabalah, within western tradition.

Appendix E

A Summary of the Forms

Forms have four modes: Mobile (walking or moving the body), Immobile (standing, sitting, or lying), Visible or Invisible, or combinations of any of the four. Visible forms are those that can be seen to be special practices as you do them, whereas Invisible forms are those that you can do without an observer being aware of anything.

1. *The Rising Light* (Chapter 1): A Standing and Visible form which raises nourishing and strengthening Earth forces, using the roots of the Tree of Life.

2. *Walking Participation* (Chapter 1): A Mobile and Invisible form. Attunes the body to the Entities of Earth, Moon, Sun, and Stars.

3. *Entering Stillness* (Chapter 1): An Immobile or Mobile Invisible form. This is our variant of the classic spiritual form found in all traditions worldwide: stills our involvement with Time, Space, and Motion. Is often used before all other forms.

4. *Bridge Building* (Chapter 3): An Immobile or
   Mobile Visible or Invisible form. May be undertaken as a ritual or ceremonial form, or
   may be done invisibly while walking. Projects
   the consciousness into altered states, and
   brings deepening relationship with angelic
   beings and their forces.

5. *The Eden Forms* (Chapter 4): A set of forms
   that can be Visible or Invisible. May be ceremonial, or incorporated into everyday activity. These forms promote androgyny,
   wordless knowledge, and inner peace. They
   also energize the body and transform our relationship with the natural world and other
   forms of life.

6. *Breathing a Room* (Chapter 4): A practical
   form for attuning a defined physical space.
   This is also a training form that leads to working with the abstract Cube of Space, visible
   or invisible.

7. *The Qabalah of Three Suns* (Chapter 4): A
   visible or invisible form, usually immobile.
   Constitutes a complete Qabalah within itself.
   A modern presentation of one of the "secret"
   forms that radically transforms the subtle
   energies of the body and brings enlightened
   consciousness attuned to planetary and solar
   forces.

8. *Ten Short Forms* (Chapter 6): These short
   forms are designed to be accessible on one
   page, each, for regular practice, and simplicity. They can be committed to memory easily, and make a simple 10-day cycle of practice,
   one per day.

- *Entering Stillness* (with chant): An audible form. Otherwise invisible, either mobile or immobile. Can be done without the chant.

- *The Crossing Form:* A visible form, with a prayer formula. Can be done aloud or in silence. This is a variant of one of the classic Qabalistic forms found in every tradition that works with the Tree of Life.

- *Three Worlds Form*: Extends from Earth to Stars, through the body. Can be visible or invisible, mobile or immobile. This is a short variant of the *Rising Light* and *Walking Participation* forms.

- *The Four Archangels*: A short form that may be visible or invisible. Usually an immobile form though can also be done walking. With practice, you may combine this with *Walking Participation.*

- *The Tree and the Body*: A litany or meditation formula relating the zones of the body and the Emanations of the Tree of Life.

- *Gods and Goddesses:* A litany or meditation formula working with the deities and the Emanations of the Tree of Life.

- *The Hall of Light:* A visionary form, usually immobile and therefore visible. Should be undertaken in privacy without interruption. Once you are practiced in this form, it may be done while walking with eyes open. (Tends to attract attention when you do it outdoors. Be advised!)

- *The Cube of Presence*: This is a short modern variant of a classic Qabalistic form. Visible or invisible, usually immobile. May be used as a ceremonial, especially when combined with the Crossing Form and other exteriorizing forms.
- *Externalizing the Crossing*: A ceremonial and visible form. Used to attune a space, define and clarify spiritual work, or to permanently and repeatedly open out a meditation room or temple. This short form is a simple direct version of one the classic forms for ritual magic with the Tree of Life. Use it often in your home, your bedroom, and your spiritual work.
- *Breathing I Am*: An invisible form. This is one of the primary forms in Qabalah, found in all traditions. Both a primary form, and the most advanced and powerful. Always treat this form with respect.

9. *Externalizing the Tree* (Chapter 6): This is usually a visible ceremonial form. Greatly strengthens with regular practice.

10. *Path Working and Tarot Trumps* (Chapter 7): Methods for Path Working with and without Trumps. These usually commence as visible or ceremonial forms. They can be immobile or mobile. In the later stages they can become invisible and mobile forms.

Chapter Notes

Introduction

1. Scholem, Gerschom. *Kabbalah*. Jerusalem. Keter Publishing House Jerusalem Ltd. 1974.

2. Franck, Adolphe. *The Kabbalah*. New York. Citadel Press, Carol Publishing Group. 1995.

Chapter 3

1. French, Peter J. *John Dee: The World of an Elizabethan Magus*. London, 1972. *www.johndee.org*

2. Charles, R.H. *The Apocrypha and Pseudepigrapha of the Old Testament*. Oxford: The Clarendon Press. 1913. *wesley.nnu.edu/noncanon/ot/pseudo/enoch.htm*

3. Fortune, Dion. *Applied Magic*. Aquarian Press, Wellingborough. 1976.

Chapter 4

1. Stewart, R. J. *Merlin: the Prophetic Vision and Mystic Life*. Harmondsworth: Penguin Arkana. 1986.

2. Stewart, R.J. *The UnderWorld Initiation*. Wellingboro: Aquarian Press,1985. Lake Toxaway: Mercury Publishing, 1999.

3. Graves, R. *The Greek Myths.* London: Faber, 1985.

4. To see the Platonic Solids, go to *www.math.utah.edu/ ~ alfeld/math/polyhedra/polyhedra.html*

Chapter 7

1. Stewart, R. J. *The Merlin Tarot* (illustrated Miranda Gray). Aquarian Press, Wellingborough, UK. 1982.

2. Waite, AE, Coleman-Smith, P, *The Rider Waite Tarot* first published Rider, UK. Many other editions.

3. Stewart, R. J. *Merlin: The Prophetic Vision and Mystic Life*. Penguin. Harmondsworth. 1990.

4. Moakley, Gertrue. *The Tarot Cards Painted by Bembo.* The New York Public Library. 1960.

Bibliography

In addition to reference books, useful Web addresses are included, as there is a mass of valuable reference material on-line.

Fortune, Dion. *The Mystical Qabalah*. London:Williams and Norgate, Ltd. 1948.

Gray, W. G. *The Ladder of Lights*. Helios, England, 1969.

Regardie, Israel. *The Garden of Pomegranates: An Outline of the Qabalah*. London: Rider & Co. 1932.

Scholem, Gershom. *Origins of the Kabbalah*. 1987, Jewish Publication Society.

Websites

www.innerlight.org.uk/DionFort.html
www.digital-brilliance.com/kab/link.htm
www.dreampower.com (the R. J. Stewart website).

Index

About the Author

Robert John Stewart is a Scot, a composer, musician, and author. He has written 40 books, of fiction and non-fiction, published in many languages worldwide, and has composed and recorded music and songs for feature films, theater and television. In 1997 he was admitted to the USA as "resident alien of extraordinary ability", a status awarded only to individuals distinguished internationally in the arts or sciences. His books on music and meditation, magical arts, Celtic mythology, medieval Merlin texts, and the UnderWorld and faery spiritual traditions have become classics, and he is the creator of the best selling Merlin Tarot. R J Stewart first received Qabalah in Britain from the influential teacher and writer W G Gray, and works in the spiritual lineage that inspired Gray, Dion Fortune, Gareth Knight, and other exponents of the Western or Hermetic Qabalistic traditions. For more information, and for a calendar of workshops, concerts, and events, go to *www.dreampower.com*, the R. J. Stewart website.

FREE INFORMATION – SPECIAL SAVINGS
Body / Mind / Spirit Titles from *New Page Books*

* Wicca *Magickal Arts *Herbalism *Alternative Therapies * Healing *Astrology *Spellcraft *Rituals *Yoga *Folk Magic *Wellness *Numerology *Meditation *Candle Magick *Celts and Druids *Shamanism *Dream Interpretation *Divination *Tarot *Palmistry *Graphology *Visualization *Supernatural *Gemstones *Aromatherapy…and more, by the authors you trust!

SELECTED TITLES INCLUDE:

*Ancient Spellcraft – Perry
*Animal Spirit – Telesco & Hall
*Celtic Astrology – Vega
*Celtic Myth and Legend - Squire; new introduction by Knight
*A Charmed Life - Telesco
*Circle of Isis – Cannon Reed
*Clan of the Goddess – Brondwin
*The Cyber Spellbook – Knight & Telesco
*Discover Yourself Through Palmreading – Robinson
*Dreams of the Goddess – Ross
*An Enchanted Life – Telesco
*Enchantments of the Heart – Morrison
*Exploring Candle Magick – Telesco
*Exploring Celtic Druidism – Knight
*Exploring Feng Shui – Mitchell with Gunning
*Exploring Meditation – Shumsky
*Exploring Scrying – Hawk
*Exploring Spellcraft - Dunwich
*Exploring Wicca - Lady Sabrina
*Faery Magick – Knight
*Gardening with the Goddess – Telesco
*The Haindl Tarot: Volume I - Pollack
*The Haindl Tarot: Volume II - Pollack

*Handwriting Analysis - Amend & Ruiz
*Healing With Crystals – Chase & Pawlik
*Healing With Gemstones – Chase & Pawlik
*Herbal Magick – Dunwich
*Karmic Tarot, 3rd Ed. - Lammey
*Magickal Astrology - Alexander
*A Medicine Woman Speaks – Moon
*Money Magick – Telesco
*The Palm – Robinson
*The Practical Pagan –Eilers
*Secrets of the Ancient Incas –Langevin
*Self-Hypnosis – Goldberg
*Tarot: A Classic Handbook for the Apprentice - Connolly
*Tarot: A New Handbook for the Apprentice - Connolly
*Tarot: The First Handbook for the Master - Connolly
*Tarot for Your Self, 2nd Ed. - Greer
*The Well-Read Witch – McColman
*Wicca Spellcraft for Men –Drew
*Master Grimoire - Lady Sabrina
* *And more!*

To be included in our *New Page Books Club* – and receive our catalog, special savings, and advance notice on upcoming titles – send your name and address to the address listed below. Or for fast service, please call 1-800-227-3371 and give the operator code #650. We look forward to hearing from you!

New Page Books
Dept. 650, 3 Tice Road
Franklin Lakes, NJ 07417

Books subject to availability.